Broken Faith

A Detective Bruce Taiber Novel

Dara Hannon

Blue Oranda Publishing
www.BlueOranda.com

Published by Blue Oranda Publishing
Copyright 2012 DaraHannon

Cover Design by Heather Heckel

ISBN-13: 978-0615696690 (Blue Oranda Publishing)

ISBN-10: 0615696694

Table of Contents

CHAPTER ONE

Detective William Taiber stared at the crime scene in anger and frustration. His partner stood beside him, shaking her head in disgust. "What kind of sick monster does this kind of shit?"

William, Bruce to his friends and colleagues since he hated every variation of his given name, nodded in agreement. The individual parts of the scene were enough to raise an eyebrow at the possible mental health of the murderer. Taken all together, it was a kaleidoscope of 'What the hell?'

The body of the woman lay face down in the center of the room. Her body was bare from the waist up but her jeans and socks were undisturbed except for stains of blood and dirt. It had already been determined from the broken railings and trails of debris that she had been thrown off the second story landing at least twice. However, the heavy bruising around her neck indicated that it was not the falls that had killed her and the apparent rage and violence of her death were at odds with the cold calm required for what had been done afterwards. The skin of her back had been cut away and carefully removed down to the muscle creating a red silhouette reminiscent of wings. The murderer had obviously been highly skilled as there was no unintentional damage to the muscles or surrounding skin and the person had even taken the time to clean the wounds so that the design stood out. Then there was what the murderer had done to the wall. Words, obviously written in the woman's blood, spelled out "You better not cry…Saint T. Claus is coming to town."

Two children had also been discovered at the scene, alive. They had been found lying on the floor, unconscious, each grasping a doll lying between them, almost as if they had fallen asleep playing tug-of-war with it. It had been a relief that the murderer had not harmed them but it was obvious they had received his or her attention. Each child had red X's over their ears, eyes, mouths and the backs of their shirts, also in blood. Fortunately, the blood could not have belonged to either child. There was not a mark on either of them though an ambulance had still taken them to the hospital immediately.

Most frustrating, though, was the fact the forensics team had been at work for hours and, so far, found nothing. No signs of forced entry. The only unlocked window was on the second story. That was the obvious answer for the question of entrance but there were no trees in the yard it faced and the nearest house was too far for anyone to have jumped, Well, Bruce silently qualified, too far for anyone human. A ladder had been assumed next. However, it had rained all day, ending at sundown and the ground was still wet but no footprints could be found under the window nor any indentations like a ladder would leave. Every surface had been dusted but there were no fingerprints anywhere in the house other than the woman's and the children's and no muddy footprints to give a hint about the mode of entrance or the path the killer took.

Nothing about this made sense and Bruce knew they had to get a break of some kind soon because this was the second murder in town by the same individual. The first had been almost identical. Only the number of victims, two dead adults and one unconscious child, and the words had been different. The previous wall had been covered with the first line of the song: "You better watch out…Saint T. Claus is coming to town."

The detective had done a search through the computers after the first murder so he knew this was only the beginning of a string of crimes if he did not put a stop to it. Four other towns this year had had a string of murders identical in MO to this one, new line of the Christmas carol at each site, and each series had only ended with the completion of the song. The detective was determined that that would not happen this time. He would end it here and now. Unfortunately, to carry out that private oath, he needed some kind of clue.

"It's not even Christmas."

A glare at his partner for the macabre joke accompanied his abrupt departure from the scene. He did not even respond to the usual jokes about going back to his cave and consulting his crime fighting computer. They were old jokes and made only because of his success rate in solving seemingly impossible cases.

However, his destination was not an advanced technological hideout. Instead, it was the poorer part of town to which he drove, an area pretty much unpopulated and given up on. No one even bothered to try to mend the broken windows or repaint the weathered walls. The only people who wanted to own anything in the area here only wanted the tax breaks and certainly would never dream of living here. So, the weeds in the yards and the park were allowed to do as they wished and were taking over the urban landscape in scraggly patches.

Bruce was forced to drive slowly through the streets; deep pot holes and debris littering the road were a danger to the undercarriage of his car and made navigation tricky. Strange shadows flitted quickly out of range of his headlights but he paid them no mind as he concentrated on his driving, finally pulling into what used to be a fast food restaurant now surrounded on three sides by dark trees and weeds, the flora encroaching so solidly that tree branches extended into what had once been a drive through window.

It looked abandoned from the outside but Bruce knew better. He was one of the very few humans in the world that were aware of the truth of this place. Abandoned by humans, this part of town had been taken over by the shadow races. Things from legend and magic roamed the streets and filled the empty houses, ignored by the mundane world that no longer believed in them. That was how the shadow world liked it but the shadow world still existed alongside the mundane and the two influenced each other. Bruce hoped to find answers here.

Pulling into the empty parking lot, Bruce quickly turned off the engine, reaching into the glove box for some candy bars as he noticed the movements at the edge of his vision. Locking the door, he held up the four packages. "Ok, here's two to start making sure nothing happens to my car, no improvements, no changes, nothing. The other two are for when I come back and find my car exactly the way it is now." In any other part of town, he would have only received odd looks for speaking to the empty air. Here, he heard the soft patter of feet as he tossed two of the candy bars into the shadows in front of his car. There were more sounds of paper tearing as he walked towards the door but he did not look back. Certain races of fair folk were willing to help if properly rewarded but they did not like to be watched. He had learned that the first time he had tried to bribe them. He had checked to make sure they were taking the sugary offerings and he had come back to a purple and pink car. To make things worse, he had been driving a department issued vehicle. It had been interesting trying to explain what had happened to the transportation division. Telling the truth about vengeful magical creatures would have just gotten him a one way ticket into am mental health program. That was how the shadow world survived. No one believed it existed except for those few like him. Humans that had dealt with it, survived and remained sane.

Pocketing the other two pieces of chocolate, he pushed open the door, feeling his fingers tingle where they touched the graffiti covered door. He had always suspected that there were some powerful things hidden in the seemingly random designs on the wood but he did not know enough about magic to tell and none of the local magic users were volunteering lessons to a human. The inside of the building was dark and smoky from the various braziers filled with flames and attached to the walls in place of modern light fixtures. Strange smells assaulted Bruce's nose from herbs in the various colored flames and whatever it was that was cooking on the spit behind the old plastic counter. All the old plastic benches and tables had been removed and the sitting area was filled with odd sized and shaped tables and chairs for the various races that came here to meet and remember or to forget.

It took a moment for his eyes to adjust and he was well aware of dislike in several of the glares sent his way but he ignored them. As long as he did not start trouble, he was under the same protection that allowed old racial enemies to be seated within feet of each other. Stepping further into the room, he finally spotted his target at the bar, drinking something that glowed a pale lilac. Walking over, he leaned his back against the counter and greeted the hoped for informant.

"Hi Tiver. How've you been?"

The lean man turned, black eyes narrowing. "What do you want?"

It was not a welcoming response but it was to be expected. Tiver had been his first contact with this shadow world and had been his best guide to it ever since. Investigating a crime long ago, he had first cornered the wererat and accidentally almost killed the creature in his ignorance. It had worked out in the end though. Once they had talked, Bruce had helped the man out, clearing him of false charges in the human world and then finding out which of his own kind had arranged the frame. However, that did not make them best friends.

"I need information on a group of murders."

Tiver visibly relaxed which reassured Bruce that the shape shifter had nothing to do with the crimes. He felt a sense of relief but still remained focused.

"What's so special about these?"

Bruce kept the description of the crimes short and focused on the aspects of the murders that made him believe it was not the work of a human killer. By the end of it, Tiver was tense again and that was not a good sign.

"Let the murders pass, Bruce. Go ahead and put on a show of investigating but let them pass. You can't stop it."

The detective blinked. This was not the response he had expected from the thin shape shifter. Tiver was no coward and usually helpful for the right price. Unsure of why he was refusing to help before even discussing a price, Bruce persisted. "I've got to try. This monster is making a bunch of orphans, killing people for no reason. I know it's only in the human world now but how do you know it won't enter the shadow world later?"

Tiver shook his head. "How do you know it's not already in the shadow world?" That caught Bruce by surprise. "You know that with some of the races, there's no way to tell them from humans when they're dead."

The human's brown eyes narrowed. "You know something about this, don't you?"

Tiver nodded. "Yeah and I'm telling you what I know. You can't stop this. Let it go."

Bruce felt the anger growing inside him and grabbed the were rat's shoulder in a punishing grip. "I'm not going to let this go. No one gets away with murder in my city, shadow or human. Now, tell me how to find this thing."

The shorter male grunted in pain and glared back at Bruce. "Let go or I take the arm."

They stared at each other for several moments, testing each other's will and, in the end, it was Tiver that backed down. "Fine, you stubborn human. You want to go die? Fine. You can't stop this 'cause you're going against an angel."

Bruce blinked in surprise and let his hand drop. "An angel?" He thought for a few moments and then his lips turned up into a smirk. "I've handled fallen angels before. Demons can be dealt with if you know what you're...." He trailed off as he saw Tiver shaking his head.

"I didn't say a demon. If that's the kind of angel I was talking about, I'd have said it. This isn't anything infernal. And keep your damn voice down." He looked around nervously and Bruce's curiosity increased.

"What the hell do you mean then? Some servant of heaven is running around murdering people to a Christmas carol?" His voice was softer as Tiver requested but no less intense.

"No, this is no servant of heaven or hell. Some angels...they fall but they don't become demons. That's what you're going against. Yeah, we've heard of these murders in the shadow world, known about them for years, but it's one of those fallen angels and you can't stop it without an angel's help. No one but an angel can stop and angel."

Bruce tapped on the counter, "So, I need to head to a church and pray, huh?"

Tiver snorted. "You really think it's that simple to get an angel's attention? If it was, honestly, would there be any stories of altar boys and priests?"

"There has to be a way to talk to an angel." He stared hard at the wererat which is the only reason he noticed the furtive glance to the side. "You know something, Tiver. Tell me." The black eyes studied Bruce's face, unsure. "Tell me and I'll pay double." A gleam of greed replaced everything else in the rat's eyes.

Tiver licked his lips and leaned in closer. "Ok, though for double, I'll add a warning. Yeah, there's an angel around that you can talk to but she won't help and you won't like it."

Bruce gritted his teeth, getting tired of being told not to even try. "Why not? At this point, I'm willing to try to deal with a demon to stop this killer."

Tiver chuckled. "Again, if I meant that kind of fallen angel, I'd say demon. Nope, this angel, she's fallen, same way as your quarry is. That's why she's not going to help."

"We'll see about that. Who is she and where can I find her?"

"No one knows her name. Only thing she's ever said to anyone was what she wants to drink. As for where she is … she's where she always is, right over there." He lifted a bony finger and pointed to a dark corner where a hooded figure sat alone surrounded by empty tables.

CHAPTER TWO

Bruce slowly walked over to the table, taking time to study Tiver's "angel" as he did. The being wore a worn grey cloak with a deep hood pulled low over a bowed head and an oversized coat over that. The coat was old and torn here and there so the cloak could be seen underneath resulting in a very odd effect. The hands that cupped the glass on the table were covered in mismatched gloves. One was fully enclosed in a brown leather lady's glove. The other was covered by some type of blue work glove with a hole in a fingertip under a fingerless black leather glove with silver studs on the knuckles.

Over all, she, at least according to Tiver as the angel's gender was impossible to tell, was not an impressive figure. She looked like any number of society's cast offs.

Arriving at the table, Bruce placed a hand on the back of the empty chair across from her. "Mind if I sit down?"

"You're not a waiter." The voice was soft and without any inflection.

"No, I'm not. I would like to speak to you. Maybe buy you another…" He looked at her glass which seemed to be filled with black ink and had no idea what to call it. "One of those," he finished a little lamely.

"Go away. Don't want you." The being raised the drink to, Bruce presumed, her lips but all of her features were lost in the shadows of the hood.

"I'm not trying to pick up a date. I'm a police detective…a sheriff, guard." He threw in the other terms as he had learned long ago that some of the shadow world had problems with more modern identifications.

The being did not answer and her only response was to raise the glass for another drink.

Bruce decided to risk sitting down. "I need your help. There's a serial killer, a repeating murderer, in town. I need your help to stop it."

The other person continued to drink in silence but Bruce could be patient and, so, he waited. When the glass was empty, the hooded figure spoke suddenly, loudly. "Oblivion. Now."

It startled Bruce and he was reflexively checking that he was in one piece when he realized she was ordering a drink not casting a spell. The waitress almost ran over with the drink as they sat in silence again and her hands were shaking as she placed the glass in front of the angel before quickly retreating. Bruce noticed that no money had changed hands and he had never seen the barman run a tab for anyone.

He decided it was time for a different tact. "So, what's the cost of those drinks?"

"Life."

Bruce raised an eyebrow but he also knew, in the shadow world, strange things could be counted as currency. He had once seen a vampire sell a car for two bites and luck on the next full moon. "How do you measure the life? You give her an extra year? Perhaps youth somehow?" He had heard of that kind of exchange as well.

"No. I get the drink, she gets to live."

He stared at her, affronted by the lack of any emotion in her voice. It was the kind of answer he would expect from the type of person he was trying to stop not an...well, "You're an angel and you'd kill someone for a drink?"

The glass stopped halfway to her lips. "Why not?"

"Because, it's wrong." It seemed so simple that he could not believe he was explaining it.

The glass hit the table with a thunk as the creature laughed. "Wrong? A human preaches wrong? Isn't it your race's rule to take what you can, as much as you can, whenever you can?"

"No. Some people are like that, sure, but not –"

The voice suddenly acquired an emotion, anger. "Everyone is like that. Everyone. Me, me, me. That's it. I had a bad day so I deserve to be a dick to the clerk at the store and ruin their day. I get to be a thoughtless jackass because my feelings were hurt by some other thoughtless jackass. Even you. Now. I've offended your tender beliefs on angels so you have the right to glare at me in anger, don't you? Even though you forced your presence on me. Even though I told you to go away. You sit there, unwanted, mad at me because I've offended you. Oh! But wait—You have your reasons and they're good reasons that justify you bothering me and glaring at me cause they're your reasons and you're so damn special just like all your special little race." She drained the glass and yelled for another one.

This time, the waitress was shaking so badly, Bruce was surprised when she didn't drop the drink and the glare she gave him made it clear she blamed him for the situation.

Bruce took a deep breath, trying to remain calm as he continued his appeal for her aid. "It IS important and it's not about me. I'm trying to save people here, innocent people. This murderer has to be stopped."

"Then stop it if you need to stop it. It's no reason to bother me. I'm not hurting anyone." The voice had fallen back into a monotone.

"I was told it was an angel and I'd need an angel to stop it. Are you an angel or not?"

The angel's glass was almost empty and there was already another full one next to it. The waitress obviously wanted to stay beneath the notice of his table companion.

Her reply was soft and void of emotion. "Yes. I am."

"Then it's your job to help people, isn't it? Your purpose?" Bruce's patience was quickly slipping away and his tone was just as quickly becoming accusatory.

"An angel is to aid and guard. Teach and guide others to improve their own lives and the lives of those around them." The newest glass was already a quarter empty and Bruce noticed a slight slur in some of her words.

"Then it's your job, your purpose, to aid me now."

The hood shook from side to side. "I quit."

"You can't quit."

"I can and I did."

Bruce clenched his hands into fists under the table, struggling to control his growing anger and frustration. "People are dying out there, innocent people. Children are in danger and I need your help to stop it."

"I don't care anymore. Die at the hands of an angel, die at the hands of a human or a vampire or a werewolf or just some stupid accident by some drunk. It doesn't matter. No one cares, really cares. Not even you. So...I don't care. I quit. Oblivion." The waitress had already made sure there was another full glass on the table and the angel grabbed it and drained it quickly. Her voice was low and groggy and her head began to slowly lower. "I don't care. Never care again." Her head hit the table and did not lift.

For a few moments, Bruce wondered if she had died but the logical part of his mind scoffed. If angels were fragile enough to die from drinking too much then they would be a rather weak race and easy to deal with. No, this one had just passed out drunk. The human stared at her for several moments but, in the end, what choice was there? Tiver had never misled him before. If Tiver said it was an angel doing the killing, then it was an angel and if Tiver said he needed this angel to stop the killer then he needed this drunk and he was going to get her help, whether she cared or not.

Standing up, he pulled some bills from his wallet and set them on the table. It was enough that it should go some way towards helping the barmaid forgive him for getting her yelled at. Human money was actually more valuable in the shadow world as it was so hard for shadow denizens to get a hold of it. The modern world required proof of ID that was difficult for them to give and working through electronic means required paperwork and even more proof. Jobs were just as difficult for many shadow races to get and keep and almost none paid in cash only anymore. However, there were things in the mundane world that the shadow denizens needed and that required mundane money. So, Bruce's money was always good here.

Stepping around the table, Bruce picked up the woman and tossed her over his shoulder. She was lighter than he expected for her size and the smell of her almost drove him to his knees but he stubbornly tightened his grip and slipped a hand under his coat to grip the gun in the holster at the small of his back.

His luck seemed to have improved though since he was not challenged as he carried the angel out the door. Unlocking his car, he dumped her unceremoniously into the back seat before sliding into the driver's seat, making sure not to forget to throw the other two candy bars out into the parking lot as promised. Fair folk had long memories and big grudges.

Carefully pulling out of the parking lot, Bruce turned his car towards home, his brain already working on the options for his next step.

CHAPTER THREE

Bruce carefully looked around the parking lot and walkways of his apartment building as he pulled into his usual parking space. Luckily, all his neighbors were normal people, inside and asleep at 3 a.m. which meant he would not have to explain bringing some derelict into his apartment. If luck stayed with him, she would stay unconscious until he got her inside and the door locked. After that, well....First thing was to get her inside.

Apparently, making the deal with the fair folk earlier was paying extra dividends. He not only got inside without a problem, he managed to kick the door closed without slamming it. Dumping his guest onto the old sofa, he stripped off his coat and dropped his wallet and keys into the bowl near the door he kept for just that purpose. Loosening his tie, he stared down at the pile of dirty laundry he had brought home and contemplated a new question. How did one sober up a drunk angel?

Bruce smiled to himself at the almost Zen quality of that riddle. Since he did not know anything about angels, he decided to fall back on what he did know and went into the kitchen to brew some coffee.

While waiting, he checked his messages, both phone and computer. His luck was apparently used up. His lieutenant had called. The FBI had sent a formal request for information on the first murder of this Saint T. Claus. That meant he would have to send the file on the new one tonight and that his deadline before their agents showed up had just shortened.

Well, they were going to have to wait on that report. His coffee maker had beeped and he had an investigation to attend to.

Pouring a coffee cup full of the steaming liquid, he walked over to his guest to find her still passed out. Well, that just would not do. Setting the mug down on a nearby table that was still out of the way, he reached down and grabbed a fistful of her jacket, dragging her up into a sitting position then roughly shaking her. "Hey, wake up time." Her hood fell back revealing her grime covered face and hair and he patted her cheeks softly then more firmly. "Come on. Up and at 'em. Time for school."

She woke suddenly and a hand lashed out with inhuman speed catching him by the throat. "You dare lay a hand on me, human?" Her eyes were a pure ashen grey, no whites, no pupils, just ash, and her nails were sharp against the skin on either side of his windpipe.

He did not even try to swallow in fear of opening up his veins from just that slight movement and he tried to ignore the part of his brain calling him a dumbass for not considering that drunk angels might not wake up well. His mind raced through several plans and he decided to go with his strengths. Turning his lips up into a smirk of amusement he did not feel, he gestured at the nearby mug. "Coffee?"

For several moments, she did not move but only glared up at him with her featureless eyes. Then, as suddenly as she had grabbed him, she let go and flopped back against the couch.

Bruce quickly retrieved the cup and offered it to her at arm's length.

She took the offering and began to drink while he took a few moments to study her. Rather what he could see of her as only her head was exposed and that was so dirty he was not even sure of skin color. Her hair was probably long but so matted and unwashed it was impossible to tell. The grime emphasized a scar ran down her left cheek from temple to jaw.

"So, you bring drunk chicks home often?" Her voice was full of mockery but he did not rise to the bait.

"When I have to so I can stop a murderer."

She rolled her eyes. "Oh. That again."

"What do you know about it?"

The woman tilted her head and smirked at him. "Not a damn thing. I'm not even sure what decade it is." She finished draining the coffee and set down the mug. "And now, I'm going to go back to forgetting the year, you and the rest of this fucked up world." She stood and turned towards the door.

Bruce immediately moved between her and the exit. "No. You're not."

She was tall enough to almost look him eye to eye as she laughed. "You think you can stop me, little mortal? I've faced off demons and elf lords. I've cut down trolls and dragons. What makes you so arrogant as to think you can stop me?"

Bruce shrugged. "I might not be able to actually stop you but you better be prepared to kill me. If you don't, then I'll be right back in that bar and I'll ask question after question until you pass out. And every time you pass out, you'll end up right back here. You move to a new bar, I will turn over earth and every other dimension until I find you again and I'll follow you there. As long as I believe you're the key to stopping this psycho, you'll never be rid of me. So why don't you just make it easier and help me?" He could feel the cold sweat running down his back as he silently prayed he had not misjudged her. "The sooner you help me, the sooner you can go back to wasting your existence in a bottle with no trouble from me."

She stood very still and tense, staring at him with an unreadable expression. Then, all at once, she flopped back down on the couch. "I'm not sober enough for this shit. Wake me when Armageddon shows up." Matching action to words, she lay back down and immediately fell asleep.

For the moment, Bruce decided he had made as much progress as he could expect and sent a mental prayer of thanks to whoever had listened that he had guessed right that she was not one to kill just out of annoyance. Taking a quick shower, he began to feel every year of his life as the adrenaline drained from a body gone 24 hours without sleep. Hopefully, if he had some rest and she sobered up more, a solution would miraculously appear. Decision made, he set his alarm and changed into sleeping shorts since he had a nonromantic houseguest. Then, he carefully picked up the angel and transferred her to the bed. Doing his best not to wake her, he pulled out a pair of cuffs he had traded three precious memories for and chained her wrist to his. Depending on how powerful she was, there was a possibility she could break the enchantments and runes on the restraints. However, he was betting the effort would wake him up before she managed to get free and slip away. Unable to think of anything else he could do that night, he lay down and was asleep before he even got comfortable.

CHAPTER FOUR

Bruce stared at his computer, double checking his report while ignoring the woman on the other side of the desk drumming her fingers on the plastic wood substitute. Morning had not brought any miracles. In fact, it had been quite annoying. He had offered her some of his clean clothes and the use of his shower and laundry facilities while he made coffee.

Her response had been to ask why.

He had looked back at her attempting to be diplomatic. "I thought you might like to get cleaned up and maybe have something to wear while you wash your clothes."

Her smirk had been infuriating and he knew that was exactly what she intended. "Do I offend your delicate sensibilities?"

Bruce decided to forego any more diplomacy. "You offend anyone's sense of smell. You stink."

Her answer had been a shrug. "And this matters to me….why?"

The detective had sighed and tried once more. "We're not staying here. I need to go to the station and you're coming with me. So, I thought you'd like to get cleaned up."

She smirked even wider. "If I gave a shit about what people think, I'd already be clean. So, you either have to let me leave or just deal with being embarrassed by being seen with me." Her head had tilted then, reminding him of a crow he had seen once. "You're really gonna do it, huh? Drag me around until you've done your little bit to kill another windmill?"

He did not particularly like the comparison but he held her gaze to show he was serious as he nodded. "Until this thing is stopped, you're stuck with me. So, come on, make it easy on everyone, especially you. Go take a shower and I'll wash your clothes. I'll even buy you new ones if you want. Just help me catch this murderer and you never have to see me again. Doesn't that sound like a good deal?"

She stared deep into his eyes as if she could see right into his head and then she gave a harsh bark of laughter. "Oh you're a stubborn one, Billy boy, but so am I. Your life is an eye blink to me. As for making things easier … why should I? I didn't ask for this, didn't volunteer. I just wanted to be left alone. I got no reason to make this 'easy' on you, Billy."

She smiled wide as his teeth clenched with the use of that hated nickname. "And I won't."

He had really wanted to say the hell with her right then and there, do this on his own without her. Unfortunately, he had already spent almost a week doing this without her on the first murder and had gotten nowhere. All the second one had given him was more frustration and questions. She was the best lead he had and he was not so easily manipulated or made to give up. "Fine. Suit yourself."

"I intend to."

So, here they were, at the station, drawing plenty of curious, strange and unfriendly looks, especially from his partner whose chair his lead was sitting in.

"Are you done yet?"

He looked over at the angel. "You got somewhere to be?"

His partner returned just then with a cup of coffee for him and a glare for the grimy unwashed derelict in her chair. "Don't you have a soup kitchen to visit or some alley to go claim?"

The angel stared up at the human woman, her features and ashen eyes once again shadowed and unseen under the deep hood that was pulled up over her head. "Don't you have a police chief's wife to go fuck?"

His partner recoiled as if struck. "You bitch!" Then, she suddenly lashed out at the seated female.

The punch she aimed at the angel was fast but Bruce's reflexes were faster, barely. He managed to grab his partner's wrist before the blow landed and yanked the woman around to face him. "Mary! What the hell?"

His partner was more enraged than he had ever seen her. "You tell that bitch to watch her lying mouth before I—"

Bruce cut her off, shifting his grip to her shoulders. "Mary, calm down. You can't just hit someone like that. Especially in the middle of the station. You want IA on you? You know that they won't hesitate to crucify you if you hit a civilian."

At first she tried to pull away but Bruce held firm and she finally closed her eyes and took a deep breath, visibly calming herself. "You're right. Yeah. Sorry, I don't know what…Guess I'm just tired and this case…has me on edge and a lie like that…Just too much, you know, the last straw."

Bruce nodded sympathetically.

The angel, however, was not done. "Lying's really not nice, you know, especially to your partner who has to trust you with his life." She tsked tauntingly and Bruce pulled Mary into an impromptu hug to keep her from going after the angel again.

Trying desperately to defuse the situation, Bruce deliberately kept his voice light. "Look, why don't you go get us some lunch while I check on the coroner's report. Ok?" Mary was still glaring at her tormentor and Bruce tried more persuasion. "C'mon, I'll even buy and you can go to that Mexican place you like so much."

His partner finally turned to look up at him and he could still see anger in her eyes, maybe even a little fear. "Yeah, ok. I'll do that."

Bruce carefully released her and pulled out his wallet, handing her a couple of folded twenties.

She took them and turned to leave but paused. "And do me a favor, huh? Get this sewer rat's statement then get rid of her before I get back."

Then, she was gone without another word.

His non-mortal companion leaned back in the chair and he could imagine the smirk to accompany her next comment even though he could not actually see it. "Oh, she's going to be so disappointed when she gets back."

Bruce glared at her and rested a hand on the desk, leaning over her, keeping his voice low to keep the conversation private. "That was completely uncalled for."

The angel shrugged. "I don't care."

"You could get her investigated or even fired with accusations like that and a lot of people won't care that it's not true."

"I don't care."

He glared at her. "How can you be that cruel, that selfish? What did she ever do to you to make you not care?"

The angel tilted her hooded head. "Selfish? Tell me this…why should I care? She doesn't. As far as she knows, I'm homeless and dirty 'cause I'm too poor to afford to get clean and probably haven't eaten a good meal in a very long time. Did she inquire? Did she offer help? Even ask my name or wish me a good day? No. She only cares that I'm in her chair and that I offend her nose and eyes. You don't care either. You only care about solving your case. Outside of that, you don't care a thing about me or what happens to me. So, she doesn't care about me. You don't care about me. But for some reason, I'm selfish because I don't care about either of you? Yeah, that's not hypocritical. That's real right." She gave a low mocking laugh. "Did it occur to you, you don't even know my name?"

Bruce opened his mouth to respond and then closed it as he realized, she had a point. He had never asked her about her name. He had just been so focused on getting this case solved that it had never occurred to him to ask her anything at all about herself, not even if she was hungry. All he had done was to offer her a few minor things and demand help. He sat back against the desk edge and slowly breathed in and out. "Ok, how about we start over?"

She shook her head. "There is no such thing in life. There is no undo button or do over. Once something is done, it's done."

The angel was not going to make this easy. Of course, she had already admitted to that and he had already accepted it in keeping her around. "You're right. I admit it." He looked down at her. "So, what is your name?"

"I don't think you could actually pronounce it. Most humans can't pronounce angelic names. Most of the names predate human language."

He decided to take her response as logical instead of offensive. Actually, it was more helpful and less insulting than almost anything else she had said so far. "So, what do humans call you then…when they're not being insulting?"

She shrugged. "Lots of things. It doesn't matter."

At that point, he could think of quite a few things to call her, none of them complimentary. However, he was trying to be nice. "What would you like me to call you?"

"Call me whatever you like. I really don't care." Her voice was once more completely emotionless.

Again, his brain made quite a few suggestions but not a one of them would help him in his attempt to make peace with her. So, he set his mind to trying to figure out a nice name. It was not as easy as it sounded and he was interrupted by a ring from his cell phone. Picking it up, he smiled to hear the coroner on the other end inviting him down for the report. Thanking him, he jerked his head to the side. "C'mon. We're going down to the morgue."

"Oh joy of joys." Despite the sarcasm in her tone, though, she did not argue further as she stood and silently followed him.

CHAPTER FIVE

The morgue was cold as they entered. Usually, the report would just be delivered to him, but Bruce had wanted a more personal review due to the strangeness of the case. So, he had arranged for the coroner to make time to explain the results to him next to the actual corpse. As they moved deeper into the chill well-lit room, he looked over at the angel in curiosity, wondering what her reaction would be. However, with her hood pulled up, it was impossible to tell if she had any response to it all.

Shrugging to himself, he moved over to the table holding the latest victim. The coroner stood across from him and began to explain the various wounds and the inferences one could take from them. The body had been bodily thrown from the second story landing through the railings at least three times from the placement of the bruises and she was most likely drug up the stairs at least once from the missing patches of hair that indicated it had ripped out by someone using it to pull her along. Her death was due to asphyxiation from strangulation as shown by the heavy bruising around her neck but the force had been great enough to crush her windpipe and actually fracture the vertebrae in her neck. The cuts along the back had been done after death and with surgical precision. The coroner was not certain of the weapon but it would have been scalpel sharp.

Bruce listened carefully, filing away each fact as the coroner walked them through every injury. The angel stood beside him, silently.

Near the end, the phone rang and the coroner excused himself to answer it, mentioning expecting an important call from a colleague and asking them to wait for him.

Bruce agreed and then looked over at his companion, wondering what to do for the next few moments. He was surprised to see her reach up and carefully stroke a piece of hair from the dead woman's face. The movement was so completely out of character for her, he could not resist commenting. "So, did you know Amanda Blaine?"

"Mandy. She hated being called Amanda. It's a fat girl's name." Her voice was soft.

Bruce kept his own voice low, thinking carefully about his next question to try to take advantage of this odd mood. "You knew her?"

"Once upon a time, long ago. Yes. I knew her. Dealt with her."

He licked his lips, deciding to take a chance. This might be his best opportunity. "This is one of the innocents that's getting killed. For your memories of her, will you help me?"

The angel turned to him and pushed her hood back slightly so he could see her face, an eyebrow raised sardonically. "Innocent? Maybe you should ask Celeste Williams just how innocent Mandy here was."

The door behind them opened, shattering the mood, as the coroner came back in and the angel pulled her hood forward again. Suddenly, Bruce found himself impatient to get back to his desk. She had given him a clue if he could figure it out and he really wanted to get to it. However, the coroner had been doing him a favor with this personal interview and Bruce reminded himself to be patient.

Eventually, he had as much information from the coroner as he could get, which was not much, and he and his silent companion were walking back to his desk. Mary was already back, sitting in her chair, when he set the report folder on the desk.

She smiled up at him. "I got you your usual." She gestured at the Styrofoam carton on his desk then she noticed his shadow and frowned. "Maybe she can wait outside for a little bit…until we're done eating at least." Her nose wrinkled in obvious distaste for the other woman.

Bruce understood her reaction to the other's unkempt state. However, after the talk with the angel, he also considered it lacking in compassion, especially since he honestly was still not sure if angels needed to eat. Reaching over, he snagged a chair and brought it over to his side of the desk for the angel before sitting down in his own chair. Opening the carton, he turned it toward her and held out a napkin. "Want some?"

The angel stood still for a few moments and he could feel her staring at him from the shadows of her hood. Then, she quietly sat down and reached over for the napkin and a taco with soft, actually polite thank you. Bruce almost blinked in amazement but decided a simple you're welcome and no other response would be best.

Turning to his computer, he quickly brought up search windows for the various databases including the general web and put in Amanda's name and Celeste's, trying out various spellings and quickly reading through the results before clicking to the next finding as he absently finished his meal. Mary ate quietly on the other side of the desk, recognizing his search mode from long association with him and knowing better than to try to get his attention until he was done.

Unfortunately, Bruce was disappointed when he finished the final search. He had not found anything on Amanda Blaine other than the current news on her death. As for Celeste Williams, the most he could find was an old closed case on a suicide from more than 20 years earlier. He let his computer rest and sat back while Mary gathered the trash from the meal and got rid of it before asking. "So? Anything?"

Bruce shook his head slowly. "No...maybe a lead, but I'm not sure." He handed the folder from the coroner over to her. "Check it out to see if you can find something I missed. I'm going to check further on the possibility of this lead." Standing up, he looked over at the angel. "C'mon."

The angel snickered softly. "Oh, yes, sir, of course."

Mary stood and laid a hand on his shoulder as he passed her desk. She leaned in with a glare at the angel. "What is it with her, Bruce? Why are you dragging that thing around?"

He shook his head slightly. "I can't tell you yet, Mary. Just trust me on this, ok?"

She nodded. "I always do since these weird ass things of yours always work out but...this? I've got no clue."

Bruce smiled at her. "Well, don't tell anyone about her, especially not the FBI. At least, not yet."

Mary laughed. "What would I tell them anyway? That your taste in dates is even worse than I always said? You used to actually stay away from the dog pound when picking up women."

The last part of the conversation had gotten loud enough that he knew the angel could not avoid hearing it and, looking back at her, he realized how much he and Mary were proving the annoying pain in the ass right. He gave his partner a short nod and reached back to take hold of the angels' upper arm before starting toward the elevator. "I've gotta go. I'll check in later once I know if I've got something."

CHAPTER SIX

It was almost an hour of silence later when Bruce finally pulled the car into a parking space and turned off the engine. He had made sure to pick a place on the edge of town, the parking lot of an old abandoned warehouse. No one was ever around so it seemed like a place to have a conversation with her without interruption. To further ensure that, he turned off his cell phone and the radio in the car before turning to the angel. "Ok. Who is Celeste Williams and what does she have to do with Amanda Blaine?"

The angel pushed back her hood and turned her head just enough to look at him. "You were searching through the computer. Didn't you find anything?"

"Very little but I want to know what you know. Is Celeste tied into this death somehow? Is it her avenging ghost or something?" He was sure the second suggestion was wrong. Tiver had specifically said it was an angel. Besides, there had never been any connection found among the other victims, so one suicide could not explain all the deaths. However, all his senses told him that her mentioning the names was significant. He just could not figure out how…yet.

She continued to stare at him with those strange inhuman eyes of hers as the silence became uncomfortable.

"Look, all I could find was that Celeste Williams committed suicide 24 years ago at age 14. That's all. I could not find anything about Amanda other than the usual driver's license and personal information like that. So, please, tell me, what's the connection between the two?"

She continued to stare at him, as if reading him, then leaned back against the seat and stared out the front window. Her voice was soft, impersonal, when she spoke again. "Mandy was a beautiful popular little girl back in high school. Already had the senior boys interested even as a freshman. Celeste Williams was new at the school. She was very shy and very jumpy. Among other things, Mandy was quite clever and personable when she wanted to be. It didn't take her long to find out Celeste's secrets. Despite all the pain and shit she'd already been through, she never saw Mandy coming. The fact was Celeste was a ward of the state, taken into custody after being removed from her mother who had been physically and sexually abusing her. The girl's father had been long gone since before her birth and no one in the mother's family that wanted her could actually take care of her. Mandy found out all of it and then she made sure the entire school found out and, once the truth had been told enough times to be boring, she and her friends amused themselves with rumors. Overnight, Celeste became the sexual deviant slut of the school. There were even those that said she had seduced her mother, that it was all her fault. Soon, the girls only spoke to Celeste to taunt her and the boys only spoke to her in hopes of getting laid." Her lips twisted into a sneer. "It was just another case of bullying, wasn't it? Just kids being kids and they can be oh so cruel, can't they? Celeste didn't have it in her to deal with this, to hold out and let them get bored or to fight back or to even petition the state to move her. She didn't know. So, she decided to end the pain, once and for all, and she did."

Bruce sat in silence for several moments, trying to process the story, sickened by it. Clearing his throat, he eventually said, "But, that taught them a lesson, right? I mean, something like that…It made Mandy realize her mistake, I'm sure, be nicer."

She turned her head and looked at him with mild curiosity. "What makes you think that?"

"Because, no one couldn't feel guilt after that."

"Yes, they can…and they do. Mandy never saw Celeste's actions as her fault in any way. The suicide was nothing more than proof that Celeste couldn't take a joke, and then nothing." She smiled in that mocking way he was becoming used to. "You really believe that most humans aren't like that, do you? Well, tell me, detective, if I had broken down and cried or if I had responded to your partner's little taunts…do you really think she would have felt guilty? Or would she have blown it off as me having too thin of skin or feel that I should behave better, look better, if I want to be treated better. Honestly, Billy boy, I've been dealing with your race for centuries and you're all very, very good at finding some kind of justification for what you do. Some way to assuage your guilt."

"How do you know?" Bruce grasped for a way to prove her wrong. "How do you know she never felt guilt? And, for that matter, why didn't you stop it? You sound like you were there."

She dropped her gaze to her hands. The first time he had ever seen her do that. "Yes. I was there. Mandy was my charge. I tried to prevent it. I asked her to stop, whispered in her ear that it was wrong, that she was hurting Celeste for no reason. I even bent the rules, appeared to her in a dream and talked to her, asked her why she was doing it. She told me because it was fun and it was something to do. The child had no compassion or guilt in her. She was too busy listening to the demon assigned to her and too busy being concerned with her own fun." She sighed. "As for stopping it...How? Possession is not allowed. Hurting or threatening a child is not allowed. Freedom of choice is enforced. The rules say an angel can defend his or her charge from supernatural threats, but, other than that, all an angel can do is try to guide, whispers in the ear, unseen, just a guiding hand." Her voice had an eerie hollow quality to it and Bruce suspected that she had forgotten he was even there, that her words were not meant for him. "And then, when Celeste's guardian angel came back...He wanted to kill Mandy for what had happened and, honestly, I wanted to help him. I was as furious as he was. However, my assignment was Mandy. So I had to fight him, my best student, my closest friend...for that bitch."

"Came back?" Bruce was, again, very careful to keep his voice soft, trying not to disturb her mood, hoping for more information. "He wasn't there?"

She smiled slightly. "How many angels do you think there are? Your numbers outstripped ours a long, long time ago and then there's all the losses, the fallen ones, the dead ones and...well...the ones like me...all guardian angels have multiple assignments and the number of assignments to each angel, the proportion...it just gets worse with every generation, gets harder, gets more impossible." Watching her, he noticed tears gathering in her eyes. "No, he was not there when Celeste took that blade to her wrists. He was with another charge, trying to free her from a demon that had broken the rules and possessed her. He did his best to exorcise the demon and save her."

"And did he?" Bruce was pretty sure he already knew the answer.

"No. The demon was vindictive. If he couldn't have his way...well, he managed to have her throw herself in front of a bus as a last act of defiance. Samain did his best to stop the demon, everything he could, almost died...but it wasn't enough...not for Celeste and not for Kate." She closed her eyes and shook her head, her expression turning angry. "I don't want to talk anymore."

Bruce did not argue. He silently started the car and pulled back onto the streets, processing what he had just learned.

CHAPTER SEVEN

Pulling up in front of Amanda's house, Bruce turned off the car and remembered to turn the police radio and his cell phone back on. The angel did not even lift her head in curiosity.

"Have you been here before?"

She glanced at him then glanced at the house. "Not that I know of but then, things change over the decades."

He tried to puzzle out the answer then gave up. "Ok, what do you mean by that?"

Her shadowed face turned back towards him. "It means that I may have been in this exact spot before even if I don't recognize it. I've been through this area several times over the past centuries, been through here before there were houses here. The area looks completely different now than it did a century or even a couple of decades ago so I really don't know if I've been here before or not."

Bruce mentally counted to ten then upped it to twenty. "Have you been to this house before?"

She looked over at the residence again. "No. Why?"

"This is where Mandy lived…and died. You never visited her here?"

The angel shook her head. "I quit before she moved to this area." She tilted her head in that odd inhuman way again. "So, you brought me here…why? Just to see if I'd been here? Maybe see if you could stir up memories to make me feel guilty or sympathetic enough to help you?"

Bruce almost denied it but she had shown too much awareness and cynicism for him to get away with it. So, he decided the absolute truth was best. "Partly, yeah. I, also, wanted to go back over the crime scene, knowing what I do now. See if I could find something else to help me but, yes, I was hoping if I showed you were she lived, if you saw the pictures of the children and the family, that you might care enough to help me."

The angel opened the door and stepped out. "I wouldn't bet on it if I were you."

Bruce climbed out of the car and walked with her to the door. "By the way, I've picked a name for you."

"Oh really?" Her tone was more sardonic than curious. "Well don't hold your captive audience in suspense."

He ducked under the crime scene tape and entered in the house. "Yeah, Faith. What do you think?"

He heard her step into the house behind him. "I think it sucks."

"You don't like it?" He looked over his shoulder at her.

"No, I don't."

Bruce grinned. "Then Faith it is."

He could hear her teeth grinding in annoyance as he turned to walk deeper into the house and the sound was music to his ears.

The house looked the same as he remembered it and he stepped carefully around the outline of the body as he made his way up to the second story to the master bedroom. Once there, he began searching though the drawers and shelves.

As he searched, he heard the angel's sarcastic tone from the door way. "And why are you looking through a dead woman's underwear drawer?"

"Well, Faith," He looked over in time to see her smirk turn into a frown at the name and felt some satisfaction, "It's called looking for clues. I'm trying to find out if she had a diary of some kind. Maybe I can find a connection with the other deaths...or a possible one that you can confirm. Maybe, she's been recently pissing off the wrong people."

"Or maybe she was just a victim like so many others." Bruce spun around with an exclamation of surprise at a voice he did not recognize. Floating above the floor, shining wings fluttering to keep him aloft was a winged man, dressed in brilliant white and gold.

Honed reflexes had Bruce's gun in his hand and sighted before he even thought about it though a small part of his brain told him that glowing winged people were probably not that afraid of the mundane bullets he was packing at the moment. "Who are you?"

The man smiled kindly. "Is that really the question you wish to ask?"

Bruce studied him silently for a few moments, pretty sure he was in the presence of an angel still working for heaven. The wings seemed to be made of light and glittered like rainbows. His eyes were the same, swirling bright colors over a background of complete white and he wore an archaic style of armor somewhere between Roman centurion and English knight with odd runes carved over the breastplate and the handle of a large sword visible over his shoulder.

"You're right. My real question is, who's doing this and how do I stop it?" Bruce tried not to hope too much that the answer to this problem had just appeared right in front of him.

The angel frowned sadly. "I don't know who has done this."

"I was told an angel was involved, a fallen angel."

The being tilted his head up, sniffing at the air. "I do not smell the infernal."

Bruce lowered his gun and put it away. "I was told it's not that kind of an angel."

"There is no other type of fallen angel."

He almost pointed out Faith who was being uncharacteristically silent but decided that calling the only active help he was getting a liar was not the best course at the moment. "So...you have no clue who is doing this?"

The angel shook his head sadly. "No. I was away when it occurred."

"What are you going to do now? Find the killer?"

Rainbow colored eyes opened in surprise. "Of course not. I must check on the children of this house then look after my other charges."

Bruce's hopes began to plummet but he tried to keep his voice calm. "Shouldn't stopping this murderer be your first concern...especially since it's one of you?"

"How dare you?" A large hand reached back to grasp the hilt of the sword and Bruce brought out his gun again. "How dare you slander my race? After all that we've done for your kind? How dare you question?"

Bruce gritted his teeth though a part of him was amused at the being's reaction after having dealt with Faith. "I was told it's a fallen angel that I'm after. I'm not questioning you. I just want help stopping this murderer before it strikes again."

"If it is supernatural, it will be stopped. It will make a mistake and we will catch it. If it is supernatural, it is none of your concern, human. Until that can be determined, however, I suggest you return to your mundane investigation and trust in us. We will deal with it in our own way and interference from you will not be tolerated. I will have your word on this." He paused and stared sternly at Bruce for several moments, waiting, and then frowned in annoyance at the human's silence. "Do not force me to discipline you."

From the doorway came the familiar sarcasm. "I'm not seeming so bad anymore, am I?" This was followed by Faith's low mocking laugh.

The effect on the angel was instantaneous. Drawing his sword, he moved between Bruce and Faith, taking a defensive posture. "Abomination! Out of this house! I will not allow you to harm this man."

Confused, Bruce edged to the side of the confrontation in time to see Faith push back her hood and raise an eyebrow.

"Harm him? Why don't you ask him who's been dragging who

around?" Well, at least now he knew her sarcasm was not just for humans.

"I banish you in the most holy of names." The angel made a sound after that. Bruce assumed it was a word but the sound was as inhuman as it was beautiful.

Faith laughed again. "Doesn't work. I quit. You can't chase me off like that. Now, why don't you just go ahead and explain to him why you won't help."

"I don't take orders from such as you, creature."

Bruce took a deep breath and stepped closer. "Excuse me for interrupting this reunion but, as the resident human, I really would like some help with this murder situation before more people die."

The angel spared him a glance. "I am sorry, human, but our ways are beyond your ability to understand. Have faith that it will be dealt with and do not concern yourself in the affairs of immortals." He took a step toward Faith. "But first, I will deal with the abomination."

Faith dropped into a crouch, fingers curling into a fist. "Try it, Shrrrel."

Bruce stepped between the angels before his good sense finished explaining to him what a very stupid move this was. "Stop it!" He turned to the male. "Look, if you won't help me, fine, but you're not adding another death to the ones I'm already dealing with. After all, don't you have some newly orphaned kids to watch over...before their mom's killer comes back?" He knew the children were safe as the murderer had never harmed a child in the long trail of other bodies however, he was betting the angel did not have the same information.

The male glared at him but put away the sword. "You have a point. I do have more pressing responsibilities. However, heed my warnings. Do not interfere again or your life will be forfeit."

There was a sudden flash of light and, when Bruce's eyesight cleared, the male was gone.

Faith was still there, however, leaning against the doorjamb with her customary smirk. "So, what now, Billy boy?"

CHAPTER EIGHT

"Now, Faith," He was rewarded with a narrowing of her eyes, "You explain why he wouldn't help and how you resisted—" Bruce's cell phone cut him off and he answered it with a bitten off curse.

"And a damn hello back to you too." Mary's voice laughed at him over the line.

"Sorry about that. Hi."

"I have got some great news for you, partner." Her voice was charged with happiness and Bruce was immediately curious.

"Oh yeah? Great, I could use some right now. What've you got?"

"Well," Mary was intentionally drawing it out, enjoying herself. "We've got another solved case. When the FBI shows this evening, we can hand over the killer and send them on their way."

Bruce's brows drew together in confusion. "What killer?"

Mary sighed, obviously having expected a different reaction. "Who do you think? Mr. Saint T. Claus himself. He's right here, ready to write his confession all by himself." She laughed. "We get rid of the feds and a killer in one day. I guess Christmas is coming early this year, huh?"

All sorts of warning bells were going off in Bruce's head. "He turned himself in and is willing to confess?"

"Right-O, Bruce." There was a pause. "C'mon, partner, it's ok to actually break a smile once in awhile."

Bruce was already striding for the door, grabbing the angel's grimy coat sleeve as he passed her. "Mary, don't let anyone near him and don't let him out of the interrogation room until I get there. Understand?"

"Bruce, what's wrong? It's all over." Her confusion at his harsh tone was obvious.

"It's too easy, something's wrong."

She sighed in exasperation. "Sometimes, Bruce, it is that easy and you really need to work on this paranoia of yours."

He did not see any reason to respond to the accusations. "I mean it, Mary. No one in or out. I'll be there soon as possible." He flipped the phone shut, cutting off further argument, and shoved it in his pocket, barely remembering to shut the door to the house as he rushed Faith to the car. Yanking open the passenger door, he ordered her inside before running to the other side and climbing into the driver's seat.

A murderer who had been happily killing their way from town to town suddenly decides to turn him or herself in when no one is close to catching them? Bruce did not buy it for a minute. So, something was up and, in a case like this, any type of something was extremely dangerous.

Attaching the magnetic light to the roof of the car, he turned on the siren and took off, immediately breaking the speed limit. As he wove in and out of traffic, his companion decided to remind him of her presence.

"Hot date?"

Bruce let the dig pass, more important things on his mind. "You told the other angel to tell me why he wouldn't help. What did you mean by that? Why is he refusing to stop a murderer?"

Faith gripped the door handle as he took a corner too fast. "He's not refusing. He's following procedure. You think human cops are the only ones with rules?"

"What procedures? He seemed eager enough for a fight. Why not work with me?"

He knew Faith was rolling her eyes even though he did not risk glancing at her as he swerved around a red convertible. "You really have to ask?" Her voice became even harsher as he cut around another corner tight enough to send all the loose items in the car rattling over to the passenger side. "Why don't you think about it later…if you survive this trip."

He bit off a curse and his next question as he pulled into the precinct's parking lot. Skidding into the first space he saw hard enough to make both him and Faith jerk forward, he slammed the vehicle into park. Yanking out the keys, he was out of the car before Faith had undone her seatbelt.

Gritting his teeth to keep from yelling at her to hurry, he took hold of her jacket as soon as she closed the door and strode into the building. His expression must have been harsh because his fellow officers melted out of his path to the elevators. Once inside, he pushed the button for the fourth floor and tapped his foot in impatience as the doors slid closed and they began to slowly rise.

The speakers were playing something canned and soft that did nothing to soothe his mood. So, seeking a distraction, he looked over at Faith to question her further. However, that thought went immediately out of his head as he moved to see her back more clearly. There were scorch line marks starting just above where her shoulder blades would be under the dirty clothes and then proceeding down her back, angling off from her spine area. He knew for a fact they had not been there when he first met her or even this morning and he demanded an explanation.

Faith twisted away from him and glared back. "None of your damn business."

Bruce was about to argue that point when the metal doors slid open once again. Reaching out and grabbing her arm again, he bit out a short, "C'mon," and led her over to a desk next to a large steel door.

The uniformed man behind the desk was obviously bored which calmed Bruce a bit. It meant his worst fears had not come about. However, he was still extremely uneasy about this miraculous confession.

The sergeant yawned as Bruce followed procedure, asking which room Mary was in and signing in himself. Then, he hit the snag.

The officer, quite naturally, looked up and asked who Faith was and where she thought she was going.

Bruce silently berated himself. The list would show Mary was already with a prisoner and, even if the sergeant had missed that fact, Faith was not in handcuffs. His mind raced for some excuse and decided that the truth, the barest truth, was his best lie at the moment. "She's a consultant with specialized knowledge regarding the case."

The other man looked her over, seeing a vagrant with a deep hood pulled low over her face and he raised an eyebrow at her very disreputable appearance as he asked, "A consultant?"

Bruce put on his best 'trust me' smile. "Yeah. One fallen on hard times obviously, which is lucky for me. You wouldn't believe how much the employed ones are charging anymore."

The sergeant smiled in understanding. "Yeah, funny how that works, huh?" He pushed the button on his desk for the door. "Go on in."

Bruce suppressed a sigh of relief, gave the other man a short wave and pulled Faith with him into the hallway beyond the door.

He easily found the room, all the way at the end, right next to a fire door leading to a stairwell and the roof. Not even pausing to knock, he twisted the knob and stepped inside, surprising Mary and the cuffed suspect.

"Bruce? What—" His partner quickly regained her composure in front of their audience. "Well, well, eager to finish up the case as always, hmmm?" Then her eyes narrowed, "What is she doing here?"

Bruce shook his head slightly in warning as he let go of Faith and stepped in front of her, shielding her from both the other humans in the room. Mary was a good partner in a lot of ways. She was loyal, watched his back, covered for him when he was wandering strange places for clues and was a good gauge for how realistic his reports sounded when he was done. When she looked at him like his explanation was crazy, he knew he needed to twist the report a bit more to make it sound mundane. However, she was not the most aware person in the world. He was pretty sure she thought he was at least partially insane as she, like most people, did not believe in the shadow world so his explanations and investigation style completely confounded her. She was, also, completely sincere in her belief that this guy was the killer they had been looking for, took it at face value, too trusting.

She was still waiting for an answer despite how it must look to the prisoner so he bit off a quick answer. "Consultant. So what do we have here?"

"Consultant? What the hell does she have to say about anything that's going on? If you want her around fine but she can wait at your desk."

Bruce glared at her and lowered his voice. "I don't want to argue with you right now so fucking drop it and tell me what you think you've got here."

They glared at each other but she looked away first, slipping into report mode though obviously not happy. He was going to have to smooth this over with her later he knew but, for the moment, he concentrated on what she was saying. "Mr. Jasper Rogers, 29 years old, no address and no employer. He is willing to confess to the murders of Amanda Blaine, Daniel Jenkins and a large number of others throughout all 50 states over the span of 10 years."

Bruce raised an eyebrow. This guy would have had to start killing at 19 for his story to be true. So, either he was a murder prodigy or he was a liar and Bruce was betting on the latter. He looked over at the prisoner. Jasper was a slim man who had obviously missed a few too many meals, dirtier and even more unkempt than Faith. His fingers were grime encrusted though there were a few spots under the nails that might be blood.

Moving to the table, Bruce placed both hands on the pitted surface and loomed over the other man. "So, you're the Santa Claus murderer?" He intentionally used the wrong name.

Jasper was already nodding. "Yes, I am. I killed that woman and would have slit the throats of those kids too but I ran out of time."

That cinched it. This guy did not know anything about the murders and, though Bruce couldn't fathom why Mary was going along with the farce, he wasn't going to let it go any further. "You're a liar, Jasper. You don't know the manner of death and you don't know the signature. So, why don't you tell me why you're trying to take the blame?"

Jasper's eyes narrowed angrily almost seeming to glow in animosity. "But I am the killer. So what if I don't remember exactly how I killed each one of them. I did it and, if you're stupid enough to let me out, I'll just keep on killing but it'll all be on your head from now on."

Bruce smirked down at him. "No, 'cause you're not a murderer, Jasper, you're just trying to claim someone else's work." He hoped that he was choosing the right words to prod the man into anger. A false confession could really muddy up the waters, make the real killer even harder to catch especially if the FBI were as naïve as Mary and believed this guy, calling off the search for the real killer. Therefore, he needed to know why Jasper was doing this, if there was some legitimate connection to the case.

The slim man was on his feet immediately. "You fool! You have to believe me."

"Look, you're obviously covering up for someone. Just talk to us and we can protect you." Bruce really could have sworn there were flames in the other's eyes as the prisoner strained at the hardened steel cuffs.

Mary was immediately by Jasper's side, gripping a shoulder tightly with a commanding tone. "Sit down. Now."

There was a metallic ripping sound and Jasper's suddenly freed right hand swung back -inhumanly fast, fist connecting solidly with Mary's jaw and knocking her back against a wall. The woman slid to the ground bonelessly.

Bruce did not have time to check on her as he was stepping back trying to avoid the left hand reaching for his own throat. He was pretty sure he was not going to be successful.

Suddenly, Faith was there between them, shouldering Bruce out of the way as she blocked Jasper's grab, her right forearm knocking his arm back as she grabbed his shirt with her left hand. Bruce felt his back hit a wall and decided to stay there as Faith used the seconds she had before Jasper could bring his arms back into a defensive position to successfully grab at his neck. Using her grip on his shirt and throat, she bodily drug him over the table, turned and slammed him against the wall.

Her opponent was not taking this lightly and cracked his fist into her jaw. Faith's head rocked to the side but she kept her grip and retaliated by bringing her knee right up into his groin, forcing all the air out of him in a strangled cry of pain as she tightened her hold. He clawed uselessly at her arm, unable to get through the coat.

A trickle of blood escaped the corner of her mouth but she ignored it as she glared into Jasper's eyes. "Come on out, bitch. You wanna play? Let's play."

Bruce was now completely confused and almost stepped in when she let Jasper have enough air to answer.

"Fuck you, whore! He's mine." Jasper's face twisted into an evil smile as he laughed. "What are you going to do? Try an exorcism. Pit your will against mine."

Faith's smile turned grim and she tightened her hold on his throat again then smashed her forehead into his nose. He cried out in pain and reflexively gripped the now bleeding area. During this distraction, she released his shirt and grabbed a pen from the table. He was glaring at her as she brought up the pen. "That'd only be a concern if I gave a shit about your host. And I don't." Gripping the pen tightly, she stabbed it into his shoulder, deep enough to pierce muscle.

Jasper howled in an inhuman voice before spitting at her, clawing at her arm again. His eyes sought Bruce's and, all of a sudden, the detective could feel something cooing through his mind, telling him it was time for him to sleep, just for a little while.

Faith stabbed the pen into Jasper again and the presence in Bruce's mind was suddenly gone as the prisoner screamed. The angel's response was harsh and unforgiving. "No body jumping. You want out then come out but you're not going into anyone else. Now, why are you covering up for an angel?"

Jasper's eyes began to glow orange. "Have it your way then."

Later, Bruce could not describe exactly what happened in the next few seconds. It seemed like Jasper was surrounded by fire but it was not Jasper, it was something else, then Jasper again then everything seemed to go dark and Bruce heard another body hit a wall which he assumed was Faith from the very female sounding cry of pain. His vision cleared suddenly and standing over the slumped body of Jasper was someone new. His skin was a dark blue highlighted with purple and his eyes were literally on fire. He wore the remnants of a zoot suit which would have made him a comical sight if not for the cruelly hooked talons on the end of each finger.

Faith was pushing herself up from where the demon's emergence had thrown her as the newly revealed immortal growled at her. "I'd kill you now but that's too easy. I'll come back later and take this human you dared to protect. When you least expect it, it'll be his hand that slits your cursed throat." Wasting no more words, the demon threw himself at the door, easily breaking the lock and continuing out into the hall.

Faith was on her feet by this time and close after him. Bruce found himself noticing the oddest details as he moved to follow the two and the fire alarm sounded as the demon went through the door at the end of the hall. The black lines on her jacket were growing darker and larger even as she disappeared after her quarry but he did not have a lot of time to consider this as he pulled his gun and pushed his way into the stairwell, chasing them upwards and out the exit onto the roof just above.

CHAPTER NINE

Bruce hit the door at full speed, shouldering it open, his gun drawn and ready as he took in the scene on the roof.

The lines along the back of Faith's coat were smoking as she dove forward, clipping the demon's knee and bringing him down on top of her in a tangle.

Bruce held his pistol trained on the two combatants but did not dare fire as they were too close together, their positions shifting too quickly as they fought. Then Faith's hand came up in a hard palm strike that caught the demon full on the chin, rocking his head back. In his moment of vulnerability, she managed to roll him onto his back, straddling his stomach as she struck him again.

Her back was to Bruce so he had a completely unobstructed view as the back of her coat seemed to burst into flames and two brilliant wings exploded outward from the burnt material. They looked like liquid light as one curved down to block the taloned hand that had been aimed at her side. The demon screeched in rage as his fingers raked over the outside of the wing instead of her flesh.

Keeping it curved over her left side for protection, Faith grappled the demon's left arm down then pinned it to the roof by driving the pen she had somehow kept a hold of through his wrist down into the concrete. Deprived of one hand, the creature quickly became overmatched and she managed to grip his right wrist and pin it next to his shoulder, shifting so her full weight was over his chest, stripping him of any leverage.

They were both breathing hard part of his mind noticed as another part studied Faith's wings, noting that they were not as defined, multi-hued or bright as the other angel's had been. He could even make out the brighter lines of the internal structure, what he might have called bones except they appeared to be made of light and were just long lines of rigidity.

"Now," Her voice, strong and harsh, interrupted his study and he turned his attention to her questioning of the demon. "Tell me what you're up to."

"Fuck you!"

She answered his refusal with a hard backhand across his face.

"You'll tell me. The only question is how much you suffer first." The demon spit at her, a messy blend of saliva and blood. She did not bother to wipe it away but let it drip down her skin to blend with her own blood oozing from the gouges across one cheek. Instead, she raised her hand and brought it down in a hard hammer fist right over his sternum and Bruce was sure he heard something crack. "Remember what I am? I know how to destroy you permanently. No coming back."

"You…You wouldn't dare!" Bruce could hear the sudden terror in the demon's voice and started forward just in case. "The rules—"

"Mean nothing to me. I quit." There was a cruel satisfaction in her voice.

The flame eyes opened wide in horror. "You're…You…"

Faith rested her fist on the demon's chest in silent threat. "Yes I am and the only thing keeping you in existence is the hope you'll answer my questions. And you better hurry up, I'm not really big on hope anymore."

Bruce moved even closer. He had meant it when he had told the other angel he was not going to allow any more killings if he could stop it. However, he was desperately trying to give Faith the benefit of the doubt, hoping she was just playing bad cop to get information.

The creature licked his purple lips, obviously thinking fast, considering his options. "If I talk, you'll let me go?"

"You can hope so. The only guarantee you get is that you'll die if you."

Bruce tried to be nonchalant about keeping his pistol trained on them as he watched the exchange apprehensively.

Apparently, the demon decided to go with hope. "I…I'm not under any orders. I just wanted the fun to continue. The killer's causing fear and anger and resentment. I wanted to cover their back."

"Who is the angel?"

"I don't know." Faith's fist rose threateningly and the demon's voice turned pleading. "I don't know. I swear by His Nameless Light. I don't know. For awhile, I thought it was you."

"Me?" That had certainly surprised Faith. "Why?"

"You're an angel, only angel I knew of in the area regularly. I thought you might be an avenger in the middle of a fall. But, then, I heard the angel at the bar, you, got carried out by some human cop. Knew from that, it couldn't be you. Then, I came to check my charge today and found out you've been here with the cop. I picked up that you're helping him. I don't want all this to end. So, I grabbed another charge and, well, you know after that."

Faith did not look away from her captive as she asked. "Any other questions?"

Bruce considered for a moment, trying to take it all in and figure out the right questions to ask. "Who are his charges in the precinct?"

The demon paused and Faith began to bring down her fist. "Mary and Jasper. That's all. No other cops or prisoners in here right now." The threatened blow halted less than an inch from his sternum.

"Mary?" Bruce lowered his gun. "What's she got to do with you?"

"I told you. She's my charge." The demon acted as if that explained everything.

"What do you mean your charge? You possessed her?" Bruce moved to where he could see the demon's face though careful not to meet the immortal's eyes.

The demon sneered up at the human. "No need to possess her. Lust. Envy. Sloth. She's an open door."

Bruce shook his head, too much coming too fast. "I don't understand.

Faith's voice was implacable and commanding. "Explain it to him."

"Mary wants him, wants to be him but she doesn't want to do the work. She's always been that way. Wants everything but wants it her way and without any effort on her part. She wants one big case where she gets all the credit for herself instead of as his sidekick. She enjoys the reflected glory from being his partner but she wants more. She always wants more. Only she doesn't want to bother with the actual work. It didn't take too much coaxing to get her to go along with me, to accept the 'confession' without checking the facts. It never takes much with her anymore. She's easy." The demon began to laugh in amusement at the confusion and hurt Bruce was sure showed on his face but Faith quickly put an end to the laughter with another harsh backhand across the demon's face.

"This isn't for your amusement! Leave him alone."

Bruce's mind was numbed with horror and confusion from what he was hearing. Mary trying to deceive him, willing to put an innocent man in jail with no investigation just for a pat on the back? He needed time. Time to sort this out, understand it.

"Anything else?"

Both Bruce and the prisoner answered in the negative, neither sure exactly who she was speaking to.

Faith was silent for several moments. "Swear again, demon. Swear you've told me the truth or I'll just assume you've been lying to save your skin."

The demon eyed her raised fist nervously. "I swear by His Nameless Light everything I've said since you said you knew how to destroy me permanently is the truth best I know."

She nodded but did not lower her hand. "Ok, human. It's your choice. What happens to him? Freedom, banishment or death."

"What?" The demon and human answered in unison once more.

"I didn't think I was being unclear." She was mocking him again. "Choose his fate, servant of justice."

Bruce swallowed the retorts he wanted to say, not in the mood to spar with her. "He's too dangerous to leave free and I wasn't kidding about no more deaths if I can stop them. Banish him."

Her tone was more formal than he had ever heard from her before. "I banish you in the name of his heresy by his name." The word she used after that sounded like ash and tasted of sunlight, inhuman, indescribably beautiful and overwhelming horrific at the same time.

The demon was suddenly just gone as if he had never been there, the pen sticking up oddly out of the concrete.

CHAPTER TEN

Bruce was staring down at the angel, slowly lowering his gun. She knelt on the roof, holding the pen still embedded in the concrete. The wings were gone, leaving her skin exposed through the charred hole that used to be the back of her jacket, cloak and the shirt she wore underneath it all. Shining golden blood dripped from various wounds over her face and chest onto the now vacant surface before seeming to evaporate into the air, the only real proof of what he had just seen. Slowly, the sounds of alarm intruded on his attention. He cursed silently and was reaching for his radio when he heard the door behind him slam open again.

"Everything ok up here?"

He really needed to go look for a four leaf clover soon. Turning so that Faith was shielded by his body and using the move to cover slipping his gun back into its holster, he painted on his best 'trust me' smile as he faced a fellow officer. "Yeah, just turns out my consultant here has claustrophobia...even in our big interrogation rooms."

The man's face showed a certain degree of disbelief.

Bruce sighed. "Look, she's a transient and you know how they all are...a little touched." He tapped his temple meaningfully. "I'm really sorry about all this shit but she's the only lead I've got. Can you help me out here? Give me a break?

The other man nodded in sympathetic understanding. "Yeah, ok." Reaching up, he pushed a button on his radio. "Yeah, it was just a false alarm. Go ahead and turn it off and let the fire department know." Releasing the switch, the man waved at Bruce. "Make sure you close the doors when you come back in, ok?"

"I will." Bruce waited until the officer was headed down the stairs to turn back to Faith. She had her hood pulled up covering her features and the deep scratches on her cheek. However, there were other jagged, tears in her jacket and how was he going to explain the charred hole in the back? Then of course there was the problem of Mary and Jasper. He had to think fast and move even faster.

Stripping off his suit jacket, he laid it over Faith's shoulders.

She fingered it as she stood up. "What's this for?"

"Because I don't want to have to explain the holes or the charring and I don't think you do either. We need to check on Mary and the prisoner, come on."

He turned toward the door and heard her following him, muttering, "What's this 'we' shit?"

He did not respond, too focused on trying to deal with the immediate situations so he could get some peace and think through everything he had learned. He did remember to close the roof entry and the door to the staircase on their way inside, however, despite the distractions. After all, the officer had done him a favor and getting a reputation for repaying favors by causing problems was a good way to stop receiving favors.

Reaching the interrogation room, Bruce carefully opened the door, not sure what he would find in his absence and was both relieved and worried that it all looked the same. Mary was still leaning unconscious against the wall and Jasper was crumpled against another wall. Getting Faith inside, he quickly closed the door and tried to contemplate what to do. Well, the first thing that had to be dealt with was the broken cuffs around Jasper's wrists. There would be no explaining that. Reaching into the coat pocket where Mary usually kept her keys, he fished them out then removed and pocketed the useless pieces of steel. He did not replace them with a new set however.

A sound behind him let him know that Mary was coming around and he moved back to crouch beside her. She groaned in pain and brought a hand up to her jaw, flinching as her fingers brushed over the bruise forming there. Blinking a few times, her eyes finally focused on Bruce's face. "What happened?"

Bruce stared in her eyes, his own emotions confused by what he had recently been learning about the partner he had trusted for so long. "You don't really want to know. However, I'm going to tell you what will happen. You're going to tell everyone that the consultant I brought in is claustrophobic. She panicked and in the confusion, you stumbled over the table and fell into Jasper, knocking him into the wall. You are going to apologize profusely and see about getting his release papers all in order."

She blinked again and frowned. "Why? He's the—"

Bruce angrily cut her off. "No he's not and you damn well know it. Now, if you do not get his release papers in order and go along with my story, I will turn you over to Internal Affairs myself, gift wrapped. If you do go along with my story, when we catch the real murderer, I will let you book him and write and sign every part of the report and sign in every shred of evidence and I will back whatever you say happened."

Mary stared at him, eyes widening in shock, and he held her gaze, letting her know he was deadly serious on his threat and promise. Her brown eyes turned dark with annoyance but she nodded in acceptance.

Bruce stood up and offered her a hand to help her up which she accepted without hesitation. "So, what now, Bruce?"

He released her hand. "You take care of Jasper. I need to go check on some things."

She nodded and looked over at Faith who had slipped her arms into his jacket and buttoned it up. "Oh, I see. Well have fun." Mary's knowing smirk was not kind, but Bruce ignored it.

With a short farewell, Bruce took hold of Faith's arm and led her outside to the car. He needed some space and time. However, he could not resist a smirk as he set the car in gear. "So, you've decided to help after all."

The angel laughed softly. "What makes you think that?"

"Well, you just took on a demon to help me out."

He glanced over in time to see her shrug. "I owed you something for the taco. Now we're even."

He gritted his teeth, sensing the smirk in the shadows of her hood as he drove back to his apartment.

CHAPTER ELEVEN

They both remained silent until they were back in Bruce's apartment. He decided he needed more coffee and asked Faith if she would like a cup out of politeness.

Pushing her hood back, she smiled in amusement. "Looking to have me owe you another favor, huh?"

He had not thought of that but…"I wouldn't mind you owing me favors."

She laughed. "Oh no, Billy boy, you're about to owe me a favor."

He raised an eyebrow in question even as he mentally wished she would give up her habit of calling him by that hated name.

Her amused grin became tinged with mockery. "I'm going to take that shower you've been bitching about. So, you're gonna owe me that coffee."

Bruce smiled in spite of himself. "Deal. Use plenty of soap and I'll throw in a sandwich."

After setting the coffee to brew, he dug out a pair of sweats with a drawstring and a t-shirt, her clothes were rather ruined after all, and left them hanging on the bathroom doorknob. Returning to the kitchen, he leaned back against the counter and watched the coffee dripping as he contemplated everything he'd found out that day.

His partner was corrupt. He could not begin to fathom how he had missed that. Up until today, he had always assumed he knew her, that they were close, almost family. Now, though…

He shook his head and tried to move onto more important matters than his disappointment in Mary.

Refocused, he began to review the pieces of the puzzle he had right now.

Demons wanted the killer to continue. Well, that wasn't surprising. The bastards thrived on pain and fear.

The angels…well the working angels for lack of a better term at the moment…did not acknowledge the existence of non-infernal fallen angels and, apparently, went into a rage at the sight of one. However, they weren't chasing the killer. Why? Could it be a willing blindness? To acknowledge the killer would be to acknowledge fallen angels…the non-infernal ones not the infernal fallen…he needed a better distinction.

Besides, this was all a side note. He needed to focus on the killer. He needed to know why this angel was doing what it was doing.

The coffee maker sounded but the shower was still running. Pouring himself a cup, he left the rest in the pot to stay warm for Faith and went to sit on his couch, still working his way through this.

Ok, he had figured out his next question. Why did this killer fall if not to do evil? Though, come to think of it, how was the murderer any different from an infernal fallen? They both killed for no real reason. They both caused pain and fear. So, what was the real difference that made Tiver insist it was not an infernal fallen angel that he was after?

His attention focused and his next step became blindingly clear, he tapped his foot impatiently, waiting for Faith to make her appearance.

Finally, the angel stepped out of the bathroom in the clothes he'd provided which looked odd on her. Though they were nearly the same height, his t-shirt was too large, the shoulders hung halfway down her upper arms and the short sleeves ended beneath her elbows. The sweats were drawn tight around her waist but the fabric hung shapelessly down her legs.

She stood for a few moments in the short hallway looking around, holding a bundle in her arms. Right in front of her, across from the bathroom was the door to the bedroom and she ignored that then looked to her left where the door to the little closet that held his washing machine and dryer stood open. Turning and stepping over to it, she dropped the bundle of her old clothes and several towels that he was not sure he recognized as his own from the odd brown and black color of them into the empty basket there before turning back towards the living room area and lifting another towel from her shoulder to begin drying her hair.

Taking a few moments to study her, he wondered if he had any soap or shampoo left. Cleared of all the accumulated grime, her skin was quite pale as if it had not seen the sun in years and he wondered if that was natural or due to the years she had spent in bars. The angel they had met before was tanned but that was not really enough of a pool of experience to draw conclusions from. The scar along her cheek was not as noticeable without its highlighting of grime but he did notice another scar on her exposed forearm. It was thick and had a twin on the other side making him think the arm had once been pierced through by a blade, probably slipping between the ulna and radial bones. Her hair was now cleared of the accumulated dirt and smoke and whatever else but he was still not sure what color he would call it. It was mostly blonde but several shades were mixed together in varying stripes, ranging from the white of a towhead to a light brownish yellow like aged gold.

Their eyes met and she raised an eyebrow at his still tapping foot. "You want something?"

He nodded. "I have questions I want you to answer."

She smirked at him in her usual annoying way. "Yeah? Well, I want the coffee and sandwich I was promised." He stared at her for several moments and her smirk became more pronounced. "Hey, I fulfilled my part of the deal. I'm squeaky clean and I used over half of your soap and shampoo."

Bruce gritted his teeth but thought better of sparring with her at the moment since she was right. She had kept her end of the deal. He quickly poured the coffee as he asked what she wanted on her sandwich. She told him that she didn't care, it all tasted the same to her, so he made several the way he liked them as his own stomach was reminding him he had not eaten lately either and he had had a very busy day.

Finally placing the sandwiches, chips and coffee on the table, he crossed his arms and looked down at her as he asked, "Anything else you want?"

She shrugged as she reached for the food without embarrassment. "Yeah. A brush would be nice."

He almost came back with a caustic retort when his mind reminded him of all the deals so far. He was not sure that he believed her help was only in repayment for a taco but if that's how she wanted to play the game.

"Of course. No problem."

Faith raised an eyebrow at his suddenly pleasant tone but said nothing as he went in search of a brush. Unfortunately, having short black hair and no girlfriend, there was no brush to be found. So, he brought out a comb instead. Walking back into the living room, he handed it to her then sat down, reaching for a sandwich himself.

Bruce waited until she removed the towel and began combing her long hair before asking, "So, what is the difference between an angel that falls and becomes infernal and angels like you?"

She looked over at him curiously. "And why should I answer that?"

He could not resist a smile of triumph. "Because you owe me for the comb I brought you."

Faith turned to stare at him fully. "Is that really what you believe? You honestly think it's all about deals like some mercenary? You throw me a little bone, a little kindness, and I owe you for every little bit?"

Bruce was taken aback by the anger and something that sounded like disappointment vibrating through her voice. However, he was not accepting the blame for this. "That's how you seem to want it. I've been asking for help over and over and the most I get from you is 'why' and 'I owed you for the taco'."

He waited angrily for her next caustic comment but she only continued to stare at him with her all grey eyes that seemed to see inside.

When she finally did speak again, it was not what he expected. "The difference in the angels is who they serve and why, not the actual activities."

Bruce blinked in surprise and confusion but was not going to question the sudden change in topic. "What do you mean there's no difference in what they do. Good angels don't kill and hurt people."

A bitter sounding laugh escaped her lips. "You don't think so? All angels can kill and even God has angels whose only duty is to bring destruction. Remember a couple of towns called Sodom and Gomorrah?"

He searched through his memories. "Yeah. God destroyed them because of corruption."

Faith shook her head slightly. "Not quite. God determined that the cities were full of evil and needed to be destroyed. He sent in two angels to bring out the one righteous man and his family to safety. Then, he sent an angel to pour out destruction over both cities until there was nothing left. Angels save and angels kill. It's the why that separates us, not the what." She waited for several moments, watching him digest what she had said. "It should be easy for you to understand."

That surprised him and he narrowed his eyes, suspecting an insult. "Why?"

She shrugged. "You're a cop."

He stared at her in confusion. "What does that have to do with it?"

Sighing, she turned away from him, reaching for more chips. "You practice with your gun, to improve your accuracy, right?"

"Yes."

"And you use human shaped targets or even pictures?"

Bruce nodded; it really did not seem a question.

She looked over at him. "Why?"

"To make sure if I'm in a situation where I have to fire on a suspect, I can."

She nodded. "So you practice with human shaped targets to be ready to fire at humans. Have you put anyone in jail that has practiced on human shaped targets?"

His eyebrows drew together as he tried to figure out what she was getting at. "Not for practicing on human targets, no."

She leaned back against the couch. "That is not what I asked. Has anyone you put in jail practiced on human shaped targets or pictures?"

Bruce thought about it for a moment and slowly nodded. "Yes."

"And they practiced on the human shaped targets so they were ready to actually fire on a human, right? Same as you?"

He shook his head. "No. That's different."

Faith faced him fully and calmly asked. "Why?"

"I don't practice in order to commit murder. I'd prefer it if I never had to draw my gun in my life. They were intending on taking an innocent life…" He trailed off as he understood what she was getting at. "The difference between the target practices is the why."

The angel nodded. "Exactly. It's all in the why."

"Ok. So, what are the different whys? Why do some angels not fall and others do? And why do some turn to infernal and others don't? What are the differences?"

Faith tucked her feet underneath her and propped an elbow on the back of the couch. "When angels begin, they serve God because they love. They love God and they feel His love towards mortals, all of them, the so called shadow races and humans. They want the same thing God does, for the mortal races to reflect that love to each other, to make this world the paradise it could be."

"Paradise?"

"Yes, as several of your movies and books have said, all mortals have the capacity to be good, to be angelic, and to work together to make this a better world but all mortals also have the capacity to be self centered asses that make this world more miserable for everyone. Look at your human history…all of those saints? They were just mortals who decided to be good and to improve the world around them. There was nothing special about them that could not be matched and duplicated by any other mortal if the mortal would just put in the time and energy. It's all a matter of choice."

Bruce decided to bring the conversation back to the topic of the information he needed. He had enough experience with the dark side of humanity that he did not need her to point it out. "So the angels of heaven serve out of love?" It was actually kind of hard to imagine Faith as a loving, kind angel.

"Yes. However, angels are no more mindless than mortals are and they have the same choice. There are those angels that fall to the seven deadly sins. They no longer love mortals. They either hate them or they love themselves too much to love anyone else." She sipped her coffee. "They're so angry at mortals or God they want mortals to suffer. They are so greedy that they want the worship instead of God. They're so lazy they don't want to do the hard work of serving God or any of the other many selfish reasons out there. And Lucifer offers them what appears to be an easier path, a way to get what they want. So they switch allegiance to him and they fulfill their own desires to the fullest without thought of others or the future. They do the same thing as they did before in a way...They are trying to influence humanity just as the heavenly angels do, but they seek to create a hell on earth instead of a paradise."

Bruce nodded. It made sense. "And what about you and the ones like you who are not infernal? Why did you fall? Hatred of humans?"

She rested her cheek against her hand and sighed. "I don't hate mortals. I don't love them anymore either. I look at mortals and I ask myself 'Why do I fight and work for these beings?' I used to have answers of hope. Now...well I look at all of you in your self centered little worlds, caring about nothing beyond yourselves. Not even able to lift a finger in thoughtfulness to anyone without expecting something in return. None of you mortals care for each other anymore...So I figured, why should I care? So I don't....and I quit. I don't serve God and I don't serve Lucifer...I don't serve anyone." She stared right into his eyes. "Neither does your killer, if he or she is an angel like me, and that is your difference."

CHAPTER TWELVE

Bruce stared at her for several moments. "So you know who it is." It was not a question and his voice was accusatory, but he was not going to apologize for that.

She shook her head. "No, I climbed into a drunken haze over a decade ago. I have no clue who might or might not be active. I hadn't even seen another angel until you so kindly brought me into Shrrrel's presence today."

He stared at her. "No one came after you?"

She shook her head. "No."

That actually bothered him that no one had come to drag her out of the bottle and he was more than a little surprised that he felt that way. "What the—Why not? Didn't you have any friends? Don't angels take care of their own?"

She shrugged. "I did and they try but…things happen. And when I quit…well, I didn't exactly just nicely turn in my resignation and I didn't leave a forwarding address. I don't blame them though. They pulled me back from the edge before and I pulled others back but…" She shrugged again, letting the explanation trail off. "Besides, most angels don't see a difference between me and the ones that serve Lucifer. It's a bad blind spot."

It still sat badly with him and he was not sure why though the scabbing scratches on her cheek and the split in her lip reminded him of a possible reason.

He was rescued from further contemplation though by his phone ringing. Checking the caller id, he bit off a profanity. It was from the police station, more specifically his lieutenant. Flipping it open, he put it to his ear. "Hi, Tom. What's up?"

"Bruce, there's been another killing. Get over there now because the FBI guys showed up right when the call came in." Bruce silently cursed even as he dug for paper while concentrating on the address the lieutenant gave him, repeating it back to the man as he wrote it down on a napkin. Tom didn't waste any time with polite goodbyes, just a quick admonition to hurry up and the line was dead.

Standing up, Bruce left the cups and food on the table. He would just have to deal with it later. He did not have time for it now. "C'mon,

Faith, we need to go." He walked across the room into the short hall to turn to go into the bathroom and make sure he looked presentable. Stepping into the small room, though, he stopped and stared. He had expected the place to be a wreck after all the grime she had to have washed off. However, it was cleaner than he had left it that morning. She had wiped off the surfaces, rinsed out the tub and put new towels up on the rack. No wonder she had had an armful of grey looking towels when she had stepped out into the short hall. She had also left the fan on and it had been airing out the room all through their dinner so it smelled like…well…nothing.

Shaking his head slightly, he focused on the task at hand. He ran a comb through his hair and straightened his tie and shirt. The FBI were enough of a pain to deal with usually, he did not need to add difficulty by appearing less than completely collected and professional. Stepping out of the small room, he noticed Faith pulling her hooded sweatshirt out of the clothes basket.

"You can't wear that." He looked at the still grimy piece of clothing with the burnt out back in distaste.

She looked over at him with a smirk. "Well, how else am I going to hide my eyes? I'm not interested in becoming an FBI science project."

Faith had a point, again, which was a really annoying habit of hers. However, he did not want her to put the dirty, smelly piece of cloth with the impossible to explain charred back over his clean clothes and her finally cleaned body. "Just wait a minute and let me find something." He went digging through his closet and finally found a hooded sweatshirt from his academy days. Tossing it over to her, he said, "Try this out."

Her smirk remained firmly in place as she caught it. "Oh, yes, sir, of course." She pulled it over her head and had to shove the sleeves up her arms to free her hands. Like the t-shirt it was too big for her which was what Bruce had planned. The hood hung low over her face the same as her previous sweatshirt had. In addition, 'Police' was written across the dark blue cloth over the chest and back. He hoped it would give the wrong impression and, just maybe, delay any questions. Though, on closer inspection, that was really too much to hope for as ill-fitting as all the clothing was. He would have to think of something by the time they reached the scene but at least she was clean. Mostly. Unfortunately, he could do nothing about the old grime covered beaten up sneakers she pulled onto her feet.

Finally ready to go, he led her out of his apartment and down to the car without grabbing her arm, and he was actually pleased that she followed without protest.

The crime scene looked the same as always when Bruce pulled up, bright, chaotic, crowded. The red and blue flashing lights had drawn attention from neighbors as well as the local television networks.

He parked as close as possible, frowning at the crowd. He really was not fond of what he thought of as tourists. They all gathered, curious and looking for information, but would yield very little in the way of help while getting in the way, especially the media.

As he climbed out of the car, he was, unfortunately, recognized by a reporter who had covered the first murder and the woman was descending on him, microphone at the ready.

"Detective Taiber, may we have a word with you?"

Bruce looked over at the police lines as if judging if he could make it before she reached him. However, that was not where his mind really was. He was actually trying to figure out how to get Faith out of the car and through the police lines without her being noticed and him being grilled about it on camera. It was bad enough having to explain her at the precinct earlier. He did not want to come up with an explanation for her on the spot in front of however many people still watched the news.

"Detective Taiber, I'm Francine Olivey from Channel Sixteen News. Can I get a statement?"

Bruce turned away, hoping a dismissive attitude might discourage the reporter. "No comment."

"Since you're the detective assigned to the Christmas Carol Murders, can we assume your presence here means the serial killer has struck again inside that house?"

Bruce glanced inside the car. Faith was gone. He mentally cursed as he looked around, answering the reporter distractedly. "Give me a break, will you? I just got here myself." He could not see the angel anywhere.

"Do you have any leads in the case?"

The reporter was a persistent nuisance but a minor one at the moment compared to his real problems. Faith had slipped away and he could see the black sedan with government plates that the FBI favored for some odd reason. Bruce rudely walked away from the woman, silently berating himself. He should have kept a tighter hold on the angel. Faith was probably already halfway back to the bar. At least, Bruce was hoping so. If she went to a new place, he would most likely never find her again. It was almost impossible to track a human transient. He did not want to even consider how much more problematic it would be to track a non-human.

The reporter followed him to the police lines, peppering him with questions but he was no longer in the mood to even try to be polite and simply ducked under the tape, leaving her to the policemen assigned to keep the tourists back.

He walked straight into the house. Interviews with who found it could be gathered later. Bruce preferred to see a crime scene as quickly as possible, get his own perspective without the contamination of others' opinions.

The scene was very close to the previous ones. There were white chalk outlines around the corpses, red wing silhouettes cut down to the muscle over the backs of the man and woman. Wedding rings on the left hands made him think they were spouses. There were three other outlines, empty and smaller than an adult. Bruce assumed that was where any children in the house were found as there was no blood in the empty areas and, in all the previous murders, no child had ever been harmed, at least not physically. On the wall was more writing, "You better not pout...Saint T. Claus is coming to town" and Bruce was sure that the DNA test would match both the man and the woman. That was what had happened in all previous multiple homicides by this killer.

He looked around and saw Mary in one corner with the coroner, looking over his shoulder at his clipboard. On the other side of the slim man were a man and woman in nice suits also looking over the coroner's shoulder and taking their own notes. Bruce made the assumption that these were the FBI agents as they were the people in the room in suits and ties.

He took a few moments to consider which face he wanted to present, cooperative and pleasant or hostile and annoyed. Sighing, he realized that it would be best for him to be cooperative. After all, there was the possibility that they would be nice and actually interested in working together to solve this case. Bruce wouldn't have put money on it but there was a chance.

Taking a deep breath to calm himself, he walked over to them. "Hi."

All of them looked up at him and there was no friendliness in any of the gazes except for the coroner, oddly enough. It was the same coroner who had given him the special report on Amanda...Mandy he mentally corrected himself. Bruce wasn't surprised at his presence. Since it had been called in as connected to two other crime scenes, the powers that be would prefer that the same people be sent. Standard procedure.

Mary nodded to him in acknowledgement. "Bruce, this is Agent Ferrous and Agent Strynko. Agents, this is Detective William Taiber, the other detective assigned to the case."

She was still angry at him. Mary usually introduced him as her partner, Bruce not William. Well, at the moment, the feeling was mutual. That she would coach an innocent man and send him to jail just for her own ambition still sickened him.

The man, Agent Ferrous, raised a graying eyebrow. "You have two names?"

Bruce kept his face calm and unreadable. "Bruce is a nickname. It's what everyone calls me."

"Well, Detective Taiber, what would be your assessment of the killer?"

So far, this was normal. Now, he just had to quickly decide what to tell them. 'I think it's an angel that quit heaven for whatever reason' would not go over very well. "I'm really not sure, Agent Ferrous. The evident high emotional state and the tendency towards mutilation and writing in the victim's blood would lead me to think the killer is mentally disturbed. However, the meticulousness of the crimes, the lack of clues, no prints, the care to make sure the children are never harmed and are kept separate from the crime scenes shows a well ordered mind. The entire case is full of contradictions."

The two agents looked at each other and then at him. "What do you mean the children are separated from the crime scenes? They are always found in the middle of it."

Bruce nodded. "Yes, but, according to the interviews with the children, their last memory before the crime is going to sleep in their beds. They remember nothing else until they wake up in the hospital. The killer is drugging them so that, although they are found at the scenes, they never experience the scenes."

The two agents quietly conferred and then Agent Ferrous gave Bruce the instructions he had been expecting. "You will, of course, turn over all information and leads in this case to us. We are now taking over the investigation and will call on you if we have further need of your help."

Bruce shook his head and Ferrous again raised an eyebrow in question. "With all due respect, agents, this is my town and the people dying are ones I've sworn to protect. According to his pattern, he's going to try to do this nine more times and, then, move on. I'm not going to let that happen. So, I'm going to remain involved whether you like it or not."

They were not happy about this and Bruce knew they would fight him on it. However, he meant what he said and he let his determination show in his level gaze.

CHAPTER THIRTEEN

Bruce had just finished looking over the coroner's handwritten notes and was questioning the first officers on the scene. The two agents kept interrupting and the whole situation was quickly degenerating into a contest of wills.

Agent Ferrous did not try to keep his annoyance out of his voice. "As this is no longer under your jurisdiction, Detective, perhaps you would prefer to hold your questioning until we are done or perhaps there is something else that calls for your attention." For a hint, it lacked subtlety.

Bruce shrugged as he smiled. "No, that's ok. I can wait until you're done. I don't have anywhere I need to be." He thought he could hear the older man's teeth grinding as the agent turned back to the officer.

"So you are saying you were dispatched here because of a 911 call?"

"Yes, sir." The officer glanced nervously between the two men.

"And it was about a murder?"

"Yes, sir."

Bruce listened impatiently. This was information he already knew. This killer always called 911 from a payphone reporting the murder, always giving the police more than enough time to arrive before the children woke up and always from either a pay phone or the victim's cell phone at least a mile away when traced.

"Did you question the neighbors?"

"Yes, sir. No one heard anything, just like always."

"Like always?" The woman, Strynko, pounced on that phrase. "What do you know about always in this case?

The young man took a step back in surprise at her intensity "Well...ma'am....everyone's been talking about this creep...how there's never any clues or anything like that."

"Gossiping about open cases is not particularly appropriate, Officer." Her voice was very stiff and formal as her eyes bored into him.

"Yes, ma'am."

Agent Ferrous interrupted just as Agent Strynko opened her mouth to continue. "I think the officer can be forgiven for discussing certain matters with his coworkers. After all, it's a usual aspect of humanity to gossip."

Bruce bristled at the man's tone, as did the officer. However, it was the wording that really caught his attention. He wished Faith was here so he could try to find out from her if there was anything extra about either of the agents. That thought made him realize how much time had passed since she had disappeared and he silently cursed. He needed to go retrieve her before she disappeared or got too drunk again but he also needed to stay here until he was sure he had all the information he could obtain.

The victims had been easily identified by the address as well as ID cards in the man's wallet and the woman's purse. Bruce made a mental note to check for arrest histories for both of them. A second story window had been found open and the bars had been bent outwards, the bolts stripped from the brick of the structure. There had been no fingerprints found around the window, again, though it was generally agreed on that it was the place of ingress. The agents had questioned the officer performing the process until the poor man had finally lost his temper and told them to try it themselves if they thought they could do better.

Meanwhile, Bruce took advantage of their distraction to go through the woman's purse more thoroughly. There were two tickets for DWI's wadded up at the bottom dated about two months previously. Looking over the area, he noticed something else odd. The bag was lying on a table with built in drawers near the door and something seemed off about those drawers. One of the things Bruce had always prided himself on was his near photographic memory. He had looked around the crime scene carefully when he had first arrived and he was sure that the drawers had been tightly shut earlier, yet one was now ajar. It might have been left that way by one of the other people here gathering evidence, however, it might not.

Glancing over his shoulder, he could see the agents still double checking for fingerprints on the bars or any clue as to how they were bent. He reached down and carefully pulled out the drawer. Inside, he found a notice to appear in court for driving with a suspended license in the woman's name dated for earlier that week. It was lying next to a bible embossed with the gold letters of the man's name. A glint of metal underneath caught his eye and he moved the book to find a gilded steel visor clip. The base of it read, 'Don't drive faster than your guardian angel can fly'. The upper part of it that he assumed used to be a classic angel representation but was now crushed as if it had been gripped in a tight fist.

He looked around and noticed the agents still talking to the evidence tech while he and several officers continued labeling items and slipping them into bags as another took pictures from every corner of the room. The investigation here was winding down and Bruce did not think he could find out anything else. It was the fallen angel, he was sure of it.

Glancing over again, he saw that the agents were done questioning the lack of fingerprints on the bars and window and were turning towards him. He slid the drawer back in place and walked over to the coroner asking for a special report on his desk as soon as possible, complete with a full criminal history on both victims, in a low voice.

"I think, Detective Taiber, that we can proceed without you from here on out. We'll call you if we have any other questions. Oh and remember that we want all of your notes and files, not just the already typed up reports."

Bruce smiled at Agent Ferrous, surprising the older man. "Sure, I'll make sure to get all my files and notes together so we can trade information first thing tomorrow." Turning, he quickly left before a reply was formulated.

Outside, the tourists had wandered off, bored by the lack information or trying to meet deadlines. The street was mostly empty as he ducked under the yellow tape and moved out onto the sidewalk. Bruce looked up and down the block, hoping to see a flash of yellow on dark blue material but not really expecting it. If she had donned a coat, she would be as faceless as any of the other hundreds of transients in the city at any given time. Almost to his car, the detective suddenly stopped as a theory hit him. Maybe the infernal and the celestial angels had other planes to go to but Faith did not seem to. She drank in a material bar. She was staying in his apartment. She had not just disappeared as Shrrrel and the demon had. What if angels like her had to remain on this plane of existence? Then the killer would need a place to stay, possibly eat, he really should have asked about the necessity of eating earlier. No robbery had ever been attached to these killings, nothing stolen other than cell phones but those were missing only long enough to place the 911 call. So what if the killer was hiding among the transients?

It made sense if his other theories were correct. However, that was the stumbling block, if. Damn it, he needed to find Faith. He had more questions.

Reaching his car, he had just impatiently yanked open the door when he heard a familiar sarcasm. "Does this mean I can leave now?"

The voice came from above him and he tilted his head back. There was a large tree in the yard he had parked by and, among the upper branches, he could barely see Faith crouching with no apparent difficulty. She was almost invisible in the dark blue of his clothing, only the glint of the yellow letters giving her away. An image of burning wings charring his sweatshirt flashed across his mind.

"Did you just ruin another shirt by flying up there?" He was relieved enough to see her that he would gladly buy her more clothing if she had. However, she did not need to know that.

She leapt from the branches, dropping at least forty feet to land in a crouch beside him, knees bending to absorb the impact as her hand hit the ground for balance before she gracefully stood up. "I climbed. It's too cold to run around with a bare back, not to mention too strange not to be started at."

He nodded in acknowledgement. "Get in the car. I have more questions."

She smirked at him. "Why yes, it is nice to see you again and I'm so glad I didn't just run off too." He opened his mouth to respond but she was already walking around the car and climbing into the passenger seat. "You always have questions." She buckled her seatbelt then looked at him, still smirking. "Well, are we going or not?"

With a bitten off curse, part relief and part annoyance, Bruce finished climbing into the car. Starting it up, he focused on deciding where to go for their next discussion as they silently drove off.

CHAPTER FOURTEEN

In the end, Bruce decided to go back to the abandoned warehouse parking lot where Faith had told him about Mandy. Besides, his discussions with the angel often got loud and it was too early in the morning to be waking up his neighbors. They had both remained silent during the trip and Faith surprised him by immediately slipping out of the car as soon as the vehicle stopped. Cursing, Bruce struggled to get the car into park and his seatbelt unhooked when he noticed that Faith had not run off very far. In fact, she had simply moved to the front of the car, hopping up on the hood and crouching, balanced on the balls of her feet, her forearms resting on her knees. Curious, he turned off the car and climbed out, attempting to seem casual as he moved to lean on the hood next to her. They stared out at the darkness for several moments before she spoke.

"You said you had questions. Get them over with." Her voice had its usual sarcastic edge but there was another emotion underneath it.

"You knew the victims didn't you?" He was watching her closely and noticed the slight flinch at his question. "Who were they?"

She continued to stare off into space. "Why ask me? You have a computer that brings up records."

"I want to know what you know about them."

"Is that all?"

He shook his head. "No, I have other questions too." He sighed. "Actually, let's get the other questions done first." After all, she was right. He could bring up the information of any misdeeds in the couple's past without Faith. The other questions he had could only be answered by her. "Do angels have to eat?"

"Define eat." Her lips curved up in a smirk and he ground his teeth in frustration.

"You know what I mean. Don't act stupid."

Faith laughed, a short sharp sound. "I'm not acting stupid. I'm being unhelpful." Her smirk became more pronounced in the moonlight. "And I did warn you I was going to be difficult, didn't I?"

Bruce sighed as he resisted a sharp retort. "Fine. Do angels have to eat the same kind of food as humans to survive? Material food."

She stared at him in contemplation for several moments before she nodded slightly, her voice soft and a bit absent again. "If cut off from heaven or hell, yes, but only in very small amounts and maybe once every week or so. An angel can not actually starve to death but, if too long without food, too hungry, an angel would become…dangerous."

"Dangerous? From what I've seen, you're always dangerous."

Faith nodded. "True, but a starving angel would be the same as a starving human. Would eat…anything available, same as a human, only with an angel's abilities heightened by need, again, same as a human or any living creature."

He was surprised that she was giving him the answers so easily when she had said she would be difficult. However, he was not going to point it out at the moment. "And you can't go to heaven or hell, can you?"

"Yes, I could, anytime I wanted…if I was ready to serve."

Bruce thought about that before speaking again. "Ok, I can understand hell. I'm sure they would be fine with more fighters, but heaven?"

She turned to look at him. "Why hell and not heaven?"

"Well…you turned your back on them…I mean that's why hell would want you because they all turned their backs on God too, so you'd fit. Leaving heaven was a one way trip, wasn't it?"

Her expression took on a regretful cast he had never seen in her before. "Oh, I'm sure that other angels would not be pleased or welcome me back to heaven if I returned and many would not trust me. However, God is not so unforgiving. If I were to return, ready to take up my duties again, I could. Even the angels of hell can return if they wish. All that's required is a true regret of leaving and a willingness to take up service again. That's the only thing that bans me from either place, my unwillingness to serve. I won't fight for you mortals anymore."

Bruce licked his lips. Well that answered some of his questions, now back to the previous ones. "You knew the victims tonight didn't you?"

"I knew the man, Travis, not the woman. She was not around when I quit but she seemed his type."

Her tone was the same as when she had spoken about Mandy. "He was yours to protect wasn't he?"

She nodded sadly. "Yes, he was one of my charges."

He contemplated her for several moments. "He disappointed you, like Mandy?"

"The last time I saw him, he was heading out to a bar to celebrate." Her voice was taking on an edge again.

"Celebrate what?" Bruce kept his voice soft, even, hoping not to startle her out of talking.

"His release from jail. He successfully got out of actual prison time. Let off because he was too drunk to be held accountable for what he had done."

"What had he done?"

"He drove home drunk, as was his habit. He liked to drink and he was too manly to let anyone drive him anywhere. One night, he didn't make it home. Neither did a young mother and her two children. They never even made it to the hospital."

Bruce blinked in surprise. "And he avoided jail?"

She nodded. "Sympathetic judge, no history of any hit and runs or other accidents, just a few DWI tickets. He'd been drinking at a bar so of course it was the bartender's fault not his. He was one of those people that actually sued the bar for letting him get drunk. Lucky for him, his dad had enough money to get the right lawyer and judge to win. Such a lucky man. He was whistling as he picked up his keys and his supposed to be suspended license and headed out with the money in his pocket to a new bar he planned to make his favorite for an all night celebration. I tried, just like I had with Mandy. But he didn't care about a young widower who had lost everything in his life. The judge didn't care. His father didn't care. None of them cared."

"So why should you care?"

Faith looked out into the darkness again. "Exactly. Especially since it looks like he married a girl just like him."

"You were in the house, went through the drawers."

Her familiar smirk began to return. "Yeah. Your coworkers see yellow lettering over dark blue and don't seem to care much either."

Bruce sighed. Well, he had sort of hoped that the clothing would help her be overlooked but it was still frustrating to hear how easily she had moved through a crime scene. "And you know nothing about her?"

"I told you I didn't. Why do you keep asking?" Her voice was acquiring an even sharper edge.

"Because it occurred to me, I never told you my name was William, yet you knew that, and I suspect that you were not lying about Mary having an affair with the chief's wife, but that would have to be recent enough to have started while you were still drunk. So, I'm beginning to think you have an extra power that allows you to know things."

Her smirk actually changed into a brief smile. "Smart, Billy boy. However, it only works on live people, not dead."

"So what is it?"

Faith hopped off the hood of the car, answering as she turned away from him. "The eyes are windows to the soul."

He walked back to the driver's door. "Why are you suddenly answering questions easier?"

She stared at him across the top of the car. "Because the sooner you get the answers you want from me, the sooner you'll stop dragging me down memory lane and I can return to forgetting this whole fucked up world."

CHAPTER FIFTEEN

Bruce yawned as he ran a towel over his short black hair. Once they had returned to his apartment, it had really hit him how long of a day he had had. Part of his brain was still going over all the new things he had learned, trying to make more sense of it but another part told him to give it up until the morning. From experience, he knew it was better to listen to that second part. Things were always clearer when his attention was focused on the puzzle, not split between it and staying awake.

He had offered Faith first turn in the shower but the angel had responded with her typical sarcasm. "Give me a break. How dirty do you think I got walking around and climbing one little tree?" She had rolled her eyes and walked out to the kitchen.

It had occurred to him then to wonder at that but he had decided it was not important enough to put off his shower for. However, pulling on a pair of sleeping shorts and a t-shirt, he found himself wondering about it again.

Hanging the towel up, he stepped out into the short hallway and turned into the living room. He looked around and quickly found her. She had opened the never used glass doors and was standing out on the tiny balcony. Her hips leaned against the iron safety rail, hands resting on the metal on either side, head tilted back as she stared up at the dark sky. Her back was to him and she seemed oblivious to his presence. He absently turned off the TV as he moved towards her. Closer, he could hear soft musical but inhuman tones, lyrical in a language he was sure he had never heard before. He leaned in the open doorway attempting to remain quite enough not to interrupt. The tune had a melancholy feel to it though the tempo shifted from slow to fast and back again.

He had been listening for several moments, trying fruitlessly to discern some meaning out of it, when Faith suddenly stopped singing and, without turning around, asked, "Is it bedtime yet?"

"What was that song?"

She continued to stare upwards. "What song?"

He sighed, she was back to this. "The one you were just singing."

There was no answer for several moments. "Do you know why you can't see the stars here?"

Bruce glanced around at the street and safety lamps around the building. "Yeah, cause of all the light in the cities. What's that have to do with the song?"

She shook her head. "No. It's because of the darkness your race has allowed to spread. Your criminals go free while your police die. Your children are raised so they think only of their own wants. A male sees a pretty girl or even just a weak one, he wants to feel strong so he attacks her. Don't have money? Why work? Just take it from someone who never did you harm in the name of striking back against an uncaring society. And everyone pulls the shades and pretends not to see. Listen to that silence."

Bruce cocked his head to the side. "It's late. Everyone's asleep."

"Not that late. I can hear the televisions and the talking behind the locked doors and thick shutters, the insular lonely little worlds. The fear. The idea was for mortals to help and protect one another. Then the street lamps would not need to be so bright. You could travel with nothing more than a flashlight and the stars would be friends instead of rare treats."

He watched her for several moments until something clicked in his mind. "You watched the news channel while I was in the shower."

"And other things." Her hands tightened on the iron rail. "The Apocalypse would be a fucking kindness. An end to all of this."

"Then why doesn't He get it over with? Why does God let all of this continue, allow all of this?" He flinched at the plaintive and accusing tone in his voice yet it was something he, like most people, had wanted to ask God hundreds of times and now he could get it from one of God's messengers.

Faith turned toward him, eyes narrowed. "Because He still loves and believes in you hypocritical fuck ups. He believes in all of you enough to hope that you'll wake up and realize the rapes and murders and incest and torture are not His doing. You were given free will and you're the ones responsible for the state of your world because this is what you mortals chose to do with your free will. Except for the extremely rare cases of possession, no one makes any of you do anything." Her face was inches from his and her grey eyes were somehow alight with fury.

He held her gaze, feeling calm, not really afraid that she would hurt him in her anger. She had already had that chance plenty of times. Besides, he would not really be able to stop her. She had already proven stronger than him once. "What finally broke you? Travis?"

"You and your fucking questions!" She pushed past him into the apartment. "I'm tired."

"Was it Travis? Was he the final one?"

"This has nothing to do with your investigation so leave me alone." She turned right into the short hallway then another immediate right into the bedroom.

Bruce followed stubbornly. "Or was Mandy the last one?"

"Fuck off. I want some sleep." She matched actions to words and lay down on the far side of the bed, facing away from him toward the window.

"And I want an answer to a question tonight." He sat down on the near side of the bed. She remained silent and he decided to try to wait her out.

"The song was written by Samain."

"What?" He blinked in confusion.

"The song I was singing was written by Samain, my closest friend."

His tired mind had already come alert and he remembered an earlier conversation, another close friend comment and he voiced his guess. "Celeste's guardian."

"Yes." Her voice was quiet but hard.

"Was it written to mourn her?"

"I gave you an answer to one of your questions, now let me sleep."

His curiosity was also fully awake now and would not let this go. "Was it written after Celeste's suicide?"

She sat up and glared at him. "If I tell you, will let me sleep?"

"Yes."

"Samain wrote it a very long time ago. The demons lured the people of a city now long forgotten to worship them in the form of human sacrifice, children to be exact. We fought hard for that city, did everything the laws and regulations allowed us to do and those idiots thought the best parenting style was to use their kids as kindling."

Bruce nodded in understanding. "Mourning for the children."

She shook her head. "No. The children were safe from the insanity of that city. The demons had no right to their souls. A child is innocent, pure, untouchable by hell. They were safe. He wrote it for the parents who gave up everything of worth for a fucking lie and he wrote it for our own losses."

"Your losses?"

Faith stared down at her fingers. "We fought every way we were allowed, including facing them down in the streets, killing them if we could but they fought back and they died and we died. Then the mortals joined…on their side and we lost even more."

Bruce stared at her in disbelief. "On the demons' side? How could they?"

"Because they worshipped the demons, believed in them enough for the sacrifices. To them, we were frightening and evil, attacking their gods. So they helped their own tormentors and that broke a lot of the angels. Many couldn't bear to see what their charges had become and fell...In the end, with the losses to falling, banishment and destruction, we had to abandon the city." She sighed. "Your race, Billy boy." She lay back down and closed her eyes. "Turn off the light. I'm tired."

Bruce stood up and made sure all the doors were closed and locked before switching off all the lights and laying down. He glanced over at Faith's back then turned his gaze to the ceiling, lacing his fingers under his head. Yeah, he bet she was tired. Her stories reminded him of some veterans he had met, ones that had seen too much. Closing his eyes, he let his mind wander as he slowly slipped into dreams, letting it process everything he'd learned on autopilot and hoping to have worked out some answers in the morning.

CHAPTER SIXTEEN

Bruce woke up to the smell of coffee and the sound of his alarm. Reaching over, he slapped the off button. The buzzing continued. He hit the button again. The buzzing still assaulted his ears.

"It's your damn phone. Answer it."

Bruce sat up at Faith's comments just in time to catch the slim piece of technology tossed at him from door. Opening it, he placed it to his ear with a growled hello as he blinked the last of the sleep from his eyes.

"Detective Taiber, you promised your reports would be on my desk first thing this morning and I have yet to receive anything." It was the male fibbie and he sounded annoyed.

"Well, it will be there, first thing in the morning. My morning." He could almost picture Agent Ferrous's hand tightening in annoyance imagined he could hear the other's phone creak.

"And when will that be?" The tone was arctic cold.

"As soon as I get dressed, eat and drive there. Anyone there could have told you I never get in before eleven." He kept the 'You'd know that if you'd done any investigation' comment to himself.

"That seems very unprofessional, detective. The work day starts earlier than that."

"Yeah? Well, in this profession, my busiest work hours are in the evening and night. Murderers aren't usually polite enough to follow a regular nine to five schedule so it's kind of impossible for me to do so." He stood and began pulling out his clothes for the day with his free hand.

Bruce could hear the other man take a deep breath in an attempt at calm. "Very well, Detective, I will expect the information by five after eleven, right after my meeting with your lieutenant."

"No problem." Bruce snapped the phone closed, ending the conversation. Stepping across the hall into the bathroom, he went through his morning rituals, smiling. Maybe it was petty but he had enjoyed annoying the officious agent. The FBI should be willing to accept help of any kind with a serial killer on a decade long rampage. If someone did the proper research, the angel's kill count was unprecedented in modern times. Bruce, personally, would appreciate any real help himself. In fact, if the FBI agents had shown any indication of wanting to be cooperative, he would have welcomed them with open arms. Hell, he would have thrown a party for them.

Stepping out of the small white tiled room, he followed the smell of the brewed coffee and toast into the kitchen, passing quickly through the living room area. A plate of toast was waiting for him as was a pot of coffee with an empty mug next to it. There was also a jar of jelly with a spoon sticking out and butter with a knife embedded in it. Pouring the coffee and fixing the toast, he noticed the dishes from the previous night were washed and drying on the counter. As house guests went, he had to admit she could be a lot worse.

He walked back into the living room and sat down on his overstuffed couch next to Faith. There was an empty plate on the coffee table in front of her and she had a coffee mug cupped in her palms. Her gaze was directed towards the television against the wall, just to the left of the entry to the short hallway but it was off.

Propping his feet up on scuffed old wood coffee table, he glanced over at her. "Thanks for fixing breakfast and washing the dishes." He bit hungrily into his toast.

She did not glance over at him. "No problem."

They sat in silence for several moments. "Decided not to watch television?"

She shrugged. "What's the point? Same shit, different decade."

Bruce finished his toast and stood up, gathering the dishes and dumping them in the sink. "We need to head out. The call earlier was the fibbies. They want their reports."

Faith nodded and stood up, pulling her hood low over her eyes.

They left the apartment and rode to the station in silence. Bruce wasn't sure what Faith was thinking of but his own mind was working over what he knew, looking for patterns and leads to better questions. As he pulled into a parking space, one occurred to him. "The first victim, Nancy Townsend, do you know who her guardian angel might be?"

Faith stared at the dashboard for several moments as Bruce fidgeted. With her hood pulled low, it was impossible to accurately read her expression. He wasn't sure if she was trying to remember or ignoring him. Just as he was about to prod her, though, she answered. "I don't know. The name's not familiar."

"So she wasn't another of yours?"

Faith shook her head and Bruce crossed a possible pattern off his list. Climbing out of the car, he strode into the building, making sure his silent companion accompanied him and mentally writing out a to-do list.

Mary was already at their shared set of desks. She glanced up at his approach, but her gaze was not welcoming. "I already gave Agent Ferrous the files in the cabinet."

Bruce nodded as he shrugged off his jacket and hung it from the back of his chair. "You mean copies of the files."

"No. I mean the files." His head jerked up but she was glaring at Faith who had drug over a chair and was sitting down. "Why is she still around?"

"Never mind her, what do you mean you gave them the files? Why didn't you just give them copies like usual? Did you at least keep a set of copies?"

Mary looked at him with a confused expression. "How could I? Bruce, they're feds and he was demanding the files immediately. I don't want them fucking with my career, making complaints to the lieutenant about me."

Bruce ran his fingers through his hair in agitation. "We still had the right to at least keep copies. Damn it, Mary, why'd you have to make this harder? Did they get the computer files?"

"No, I didn't know your password. You changed it recently without telling me. I'm hurt by that, Bruce, I really am."

He had actually meant to tell her. However, he had changed it right before being called to the site of Mandy's death and it had slipped his mind. If he still trusted her, he would have felt bad about that. Now, though, he was grateful for that small piece of forgetfulness. Sighing, he turned towards his computer. "Fine, I'll just copy them to disk, no big deal."

Mary stared at him across their desks. "Aren't you going to give me your password?"

He shook his head distractedly, reaching into the middle drawer on his left side and sliding out two empty CD's, his exact movements shielded by the desk.

"What? We always know each other's passwords."

Bruce shrugged and slid a CD into the drive while laying the other CD on top of the tower. Right clicking on the Saint T. Claus file icon and choosing copy to drive.

Mary leaned forward, her voice dropping to an angry hiss. "What the hell? We're partners. We're supposed to trust each other."

Bruce gave a genuine curse then a false accusation. "Damn drive, acting up now." He leaned over and hit the eject button, taking out the CD and studying it. "Should work." Leaning down further, he acted as if he were fiddling with the connections to cover up slipping in the other the other blank CD and setting the burned one on top of the tower. "There, think that's it." He sat up and clicked the proper choices to burn the other CD.

"Bruce," Mary's voice was harsher with rising anger. "I said we're supposed to trust each other."

Bruce met her accusing gaze with his own icy stare. "How can I trust a partner who would knowingly put an innocent man in jail?"

Her brown eyes sparked in indignation and rage. "You saw him! He wasn't an innocent; he was a life long criminal. He was guilty of something."

Bruce hit the eject button for the drive but picked up the CD from the top of the tower, allowing the second one to slide back into the machine. "Maybe, maybe not. But he was innocent of being Saint T. Claus. Jailing him would have closed the case until who knows how many more bodies stacked up. What would you have said then? Copycat killer? Hoped it started again somewhere else? All investigation would have been back to square one and a guy who might not have ever killed anyone in his life would be on death row." He held out the disk to her. "Now, go ahead and take this to the fibbies. I promised you all of the credit and I keep my promises."

Her body was tense with rage as she took the disk and stalked off and part of Bruce mourned the loss of the friendship. However, another part of him wondered if the Mary he had called partner had every really existed or not.

CHAPTER SEVENTEEN

With Mary gone, Bruce pushed aside worries about what Jasper might be doing to the back of his mind and got down to some real work. Pulling up the list of victims he had compiled through his earlier research, he began to run searches on their names through law enforcement databases as well as through the Internet. Each time something popped up, he copied and pasted either the information or link as appropriate under the relevant name. It did not surprise him when, after an hour, most of the names had items attached to them. Quickly saving it to the disc still in the computer, he called up a map program, setting the parameters wide enough to contain all three of the murder sites in the city. Sending it to the printer, he pulled up the local listings for any place that fed the homeless. Using red for the crime scenes and blue for the soup kitchens, Bruce marked out each location, hoping a pattern might emerge.

He was setting the last points when the phone rang though he ignored it. There was no one that would call the phone that sat along the centerline of the two desks that he would want to talk to right now. Mary had returned awhile ago, though without a greeting, and grabbed the receiver on the fifth ring.

"Detective Arbor and Taiber's desk." Her tone suddenly became more accommodating after a pause for the caller to be identified. "Yes, sir. We'll be right there." She hung up the phone more gently than she had answered it and Bruce wasn't surprised at her announcement. "The lieutenant wants to see us."

Bruce nodded. "Go ahead, I'll be there in a moment."

"He said now."

Bruce glanced up at her annoyed tone. "I just need to finish this. I'll be right there.'

Brown eyes darkened in irritation, Mary stalked away.

As soon as she was several desks away, Bruce reached down to eject the disc. Folding up the map, he slipped it and the CD into an inner pocket of his jacket. He was ready.

However, as he stood, he came face to face with a problem. What was he going to do with Faith? He couldn't take her into the lieutenant's office and leaving her standing outside would look too suspicious. Unfortunately, he was still not comfortable letting her out of his reach but he didn't see any options.

He stared hard at her. "Can I trust you to wait for me right here?"

She smirked out of the shadows of her hood. "You can trust me if you choose. However, the real question is: Do you trust me?"

Bruce considered for a few moments. She hadn't run yet. She had had her chances but she was still here. Deciding, he nodded. "Stay here. I'll be back soon."

Shrugging, she slouched in the chair as he walked away.

Quickly arriving at the lieutenant's door, he took a deep breath before entering. The lieutenant did not look happy as he greeted the detective with a short command to sit down. Bruce immediately complied, sitting in the indicated seat in front of the large metal desk, next to Mary. A quick glance to his left revealed his partner was still annoyed. Her face was set as she stared straight ahead at the lieutenant.

Bruce focused on his superior. Lieutenant Spyden had his blond head bent over an open file seeming to ignore his two subordinates. Bruce spent the time looking beyond the man to the back wall of the office, idly reading the newspaper clippings posted there. It looked like Spyden had cut out every headline indicating a successful conviction from this department. The dates went back several years; possibly even to before Spyden had achieved his current rank. Bruce had barely noticed the board before on the rare occasions he had previously been in the office but now it suddenly sparked his curiosity.

He did not have further time to reflect however. Out of the corner of his eye, he caught the lifting of Spyden's head and returned his full attention to the officer just in time to meet the man's hazel eyes. Spyden stared at him for a moment then at Mary then back to the folder on his desk.

Bruce recognized the technique. Spyden wanted them nervous before he began his questions so he was making them wait and wonder. Yes, he knew what the lieutenant was doing but it didn't make the waiting easier.

Finally, Spyden looked up again, his eyes flicking back and forth between the two detectives. "So, who wants to explain?"

It was another technique Bruce had used himself, throwing out the nebulous accusation and waiting to see if it spawned a confession. Mary remained silent so Bruce decided he would bite. Better to get this over with. "Explain what, sir?" However, he was not going to confess to anything without knowing what it was he was being accused of first.

"This." The lieutenant tapped the file on his desk and both Mary and Bruce leaned forward to look. It was a criminal record and it was titled Jasper Cordova.

Several reasons for the file to be on the desk flashed through Bruce's head. None of them were good. However, he was still not going to confess without an accusation. "I'm not sure I understand what you would like explained, sir." He made sure to keep his voice calm and respectful.

Spyden's hazel eyes became hard with annoyance. "Don't play dumb with me, Bruce, it doesn't suit you. Mr. Jasper Cordova who has a sheet a mile long gets arrested as the Saint T. Claus killer with a full confession then gets released less than two hours later. Why?"

Bruce barely restrained himself from glaring over at Mary and, instead, focused on remaining calm. "It was a false confession. Once questioned, it was clear that he didn't know anything about the crimes outside of the media. He was just looking for attention or something similar."

"And you didn't figure this out until after the arrest?" The lieutenant stared hard at him. "That's not like you. So, you want to tell me what really happened?"

Bruce's thoughts raced. He was not sure how he felt towards Mary anymore. He did not trust her. However, he had promised that she could be the hero of this case and he was used to sharing the credit with her. They always covered for each other and signed all the reports together. It had never bothered him. It was just how the work was split. She covered for him and watched his back when his investigations took him on odd tangents and he had made sure to get the right collar. It was simple. He wasn't going to throw her under the bus now. "It was an error. As you mentioned, there was the full confession—"

"Which you just said was obviously false." Spyden stared hard at him. "Don't try to fool me on this, Bruce. You've been in this department for five years and, in all that time, you've never released anyone you've arrested. You're always damn sure before you apply handcuffs. So what happened here?" They stared at each other as the detective's mind raced.

However, it was Mary who answered, surprising them both. "I'm the one that did the arrest."

Spyden raised an eyebrow and even Bruce's eyes widened. "Since when do the two of you split arrests?"

She looked from Spyden to Bruce and back before answering. "Well, it just seemed…I mean, Bruce wasn't there… he was—"

Bruce cut her off. "I was pursuing another lead while Mary was following up on some leads here."

Mary nodded in agreement. "I wasn't sure about him but I wanted to make sure to hold him here until we could question him together, just in case."

Spyden stared from one to the other and Bruce kept his face impassive. "You're sure that he was innocent? Like I said before, he has a sheet a mile long. He's been in and out of jails since he was a juvenile. He's a habitual offender and a drifter. He fits the profile of a serial killer, drifting from town to town, no attachments, history of drug abuse and even violence. So what makes you so sure? Drugs might have hazed out the details."

Bruce nodded. "I understand that, sir. However, if he had been on enough drugs to forget the details then he was on too many to have done the professional job Saint T. Claus is doing. This killer is no drug user. He's too good, doesn't make mistakes. An addict can't do that."

The lieutenant looked over at Mary. "And you agree."

"Completely, sir. I was only holding him just in case he had some extra information. He didn't so we let him go."

Bruce nodded his agreement. It felt good to have the Mary he remembered on his side backing him up, again.

CHAPTER EIGHTEEN

Once Mary and Bruce were on the same page, the interview with the lieutenant did not last long and they were soon leaving his office to return to their desks. Though having Mary's help again was comfortable, it did not feel like old times. There had been too large a break in the trust for it to be restored quickly. Still, it was nice for the moment.

Then they reached their desks and the moment was over.

"He had a point though, Bruce. You don't know what Jasper could be doing out there now. He could even be beating someone up or killing them for their wallet."

Bruce shook his head. "He was not the Saint T. Claus killer."

Mary's tone became long suffering. "Yes, thank you. I think we've established that now. You can go ahead and drop the 'I told you so's. However, didn't you hear what the lieutenant said? That guy's got a history of violence and drug use and you and I both know what that leads to. You put him back on the street without looking for what else he could have done."

Bruce turned to glare at her in annoyance. "Is that what you want us to do? Go find a likely suspect and then look for a crime to pin to him? Is that going to clean up the streets?"

She met his glare with one of her own. "It might."

"But it wouldn't be right. I'm not going to lock somebody up for what they might have done. That makes me judge and jury and I don't have that right." He hardened his expression. "And neither do you."

Mary sneered at him. "Fine, Mr. Honorable, and when we bring him in for breaking some guy's head to get his wallet for his next hit…well that won't be your fault either, will it?" She turned to leave then noticed Faith, the angel's head resting on her arms folded on top of the desk, apparently asleep. "And will you get rid of that trash already? What the hell does she have on you anyway?" Mary's dark eyes turned colder. "Or what does she do for you?"

Bruce's teeth clenched in anger. "Leave it alone, Mary, it doesn't concern you."

"You got that right. I'm going to go home and take a nice long bath before we get called in again because of your shitty attitude with the FBI." Without further words of goodbye, she stalked away.

Sitting down, Bruce brought up his screens again trying to appear calm. Unfortunately, some of Mary's words did bother him. What would he do if the next murder case that crossed his desk did involve Jasper? He had let an addict with a history of violence back out onto the streets. However, he did not believe he was wrong. There had not been any charges to hold him on. Other than being demon possessed and he just did not have the proper forms to charge someone with that.

Bruce paused. Had he made a larger mistake than he realized? The man had been demon possessed. How evil did he have to be for that to have happened? Or did he even have to be evil? Faith had mentioned before about a little girl being possessed but had also said children were innocent and unclaimable by hell. Had he made a mistake?

He looked over at Faith and found her head lifted, shadowed eyes focused on him. "You wondering how responsible you are for another's actions?"

"No." He shook his head. "Not really."

Faith nodded, keeping her voice low. "Good. Everyone is responsible for themselves only. No matter how much all of you mortals want to blame each other."

He stared at her for a few moments then came to a decision. "Come on."

She remained seated. "More questions?"

"Yeah and I thought it'd be nice to talk about it over lunch."

"Lunch? You hungry already? Breakfast wasn't that long ago."

Bruce sighed. "Fine, then over coffee."

"How about over a drink?" She smirked up at him.

He kept his voice as hard as his expression "Not until after I stop the killer. Now come on."

She remained seated. "You just don't want anyone to hear you talk crazy to the crazy person. I wonder what you'd do if I decided to just cause a scene right here."

"I'd patiently let you finish and tell everyone it's your medications. It wouldn't be enough to make me let you out of my sight. I don't care about a little embarrassment. What about you?"

"I don't give a shit about it either. Do you think I'd run around drunk and messed up like this if I did?"

He shook his head. "True but the longer you sit on your ass giving me a hard time, the longer this damn case is going to take and the longer you can't drink and have to put up with all this mortal bullshit." His smile turned into one of triumph as she stood up though it was short lived.

"You know, Billy boy, just remember one thing. Once this case is over, I won't have anything to do except drink…or maybe make you my own personal project for the rest of your life." She smirked back at him. "And maybe beyond."

CHAPTER NINETEEN

Bruce chose a coffee shop with outdoor seating that faced along one of the city parks. The stores along this street kept the trees and benches well tended and freshly painted as best they could. Unfortunately, a fresh red tag proved that there were still those that did not appreciate the effort or cost. Sitting down across from Faith, he placed a cup in front of her. She turned her head from watching the birds.

"What's this?"

"It's a coffee, black."

She nodded. "Observant."

"Sometimes."

She took a sip of the hot liquid. "What's the question this time?"

"Possession. How easy is it?"

The angel raised her hooded head. "I thought you said the killer was an angel, not possessed."

"According to my facts, the killer is."

"Your facts?" He could almost see her raise a sardonic eyebrow in the shadows of her hood. "Have you ever considered double checking these facts?"

Bruce shook his head. "No. I trust the source."

"Then why am I sitting here and not this miraculous source if this source knows so damn much?" She managed to add volumes of sarcasm into each usage of the word source.

"Because he told me everything he would. He's more scared of the killer than in need of money. So, he gave me you." Bruce was careful to avoid Tiver's name. It would be a poor repayment to the wererat to basically sic Faith on him just because he had helped Bruce as best he could. "How easy is possession?"

She held the cup and studied him. Bruce felt the familiar sensation that she was looking through him. "It's not easy. Demons that can do it are extremely rare."

"Demons? So angels can't?"

Faith took a slow sip and tilted her head slightly in consideration. "In theory, an angel could possibly do it but I've never heard of it even being attempted."

"But it's possible?"

She shrugged. "I don't know." He glared at her and he could feel her glaring back. "I'm not all knowing Billy boy. That's God, not me. I really don't know."

He sighed and took a long drink of his own coffee. "Ok, then explain how it's technically possible but not done? And how strong is it? How evil does the victim have to be or how innocent?"

"You're worried about Jasper, aren't you?" She gave a low bark of laughter. "Think you let loose a monster even without the demon at home?"

He shifted a bit as he ground his teeth. "Maybe, but I'm also confused. You said children were untouchable by hell but a girl Samain protected killed herself while possessed. The demon said he'd been hearing things and talking with Mary. How? She doesn't believe in anything not strictly normal. So was he invisible, a shapeshifter?" The thought of either made Bruce's blood run cold. If the demon was capable of either, then why not an angel? Either would make the detective's job nearly impossible, same with possession. How would he catch the killer much less prove it if the angel could hide inside another?

Faith stared at him for a long silent moment. "You're so close and so off."

Bruce gritted his teeth against angry words. "Then explain it to me, damn it." She continued to regard him silently. "If you don't tell me, then my ignorance is your fault. You know that, right?"

"You are not my fault." Faith's fingers tightened slightly, threatening to break the Styrofoam cup.

"I'm not saying I am. But if you withhold teaching then my ignorance is. Angel." He put emphasis on the last word. He could feel the heat of the anger in her gaze and he wondered if he had pushed too far, if her wings were burning through another shirt even now.

With exaggerated care, Faith released the cup and clasped her fingers together. "Fine. Angels are not mortal. Neither are demons. Not only can we exist on different...I guess planes would be the easiest description for you to understand...we are aware of this and shift at will."

"Planes? Like heaven and hell."

"That is two of them, yes, but not fully. It's a different experience of existence...mortals also exist on different planes, in different ways. There is this physical world and feeling and awareness and then there's the spirit. Your soul is not physical but it is part of you. It's just in a different plane. Mortals just can not really shift their awareness. You're too tied to this physical world. Angels and demons are from outside of this world completely. We only exist in one plane at any time. Most of the time, when we watch our charges, we exist on the soul plane. We see our charge's souls not the physical. We don't see the surrounding world except through the mortal's perceptions, through their thoughts. It's all filtered through your experiences. We only know what city you are in physically if you think of the city. It allows us to see your memories, thoughts, and habits and allows us to communicate. There, we can whisper advice without mortals fully realizing we are there or what is happening."

"So you sneak into the mind and take control?" Bruce was struggling to understand the concept.

"No. If we did that then there would be no free will and no responsibility." Bruce still did not understand. "Ok...think of it this way. When you were a child, did you ever have an experience when you were standing in a store and you wanted candy and you had this little brief thought: No one's looking. They won't miss just one piece. And then you decided that it was wrong and you pushed it away or you thought it was ok and you took it. Or have you ever been walking down a road and see a piece of litter, some little thing, and the thought occurs: You know it wouldn't take that much to just put it in the trash can right there. Then you decided to follow that little thought or not. That's what we do. That's all we're allowed to do. Whisper. We see something through your eyes that you're noticing and if the angel sees a potential for good, we whisper a suggestion to do it. If the demon sees a potential for bad, they whisper the suggestion to do it. Then you decide what to do. The decision is still the mortal's alone. Force or coercion is forbidden to the angels and the demons."

Bruce could not suppress a sneer. "And the demons obey of course."

She shook her head. "They don't want to but, again, it's not that easy. The law of no coercion was put down by God and free will was given to mortals by God. He's not stupid. He would not set down a law with no way to enforce it. Free will is a strong thing, Bruce, stronger than you mortals believe. Even when the demons push, even when an angel tries to push, it's the equivalent of your mother nagging you. We can argue and yell but we can't force...mostly. This is where possession comes in. Possession is an abuse of this way of communicating with mortals. Possession is done through this connection. The immortal sets his or her will against a mortal's and wins. It is not easy to do and it is a rare demon that has the power of will to do it."

Bruce sipped his coffee as he tried to fit it into what he already understood. "And the girl that was possessed? You said children—"

She cut him off impatiently. "I said infants. The girl was fourteen…old enough to have temptations, old enough to make actual decisions. Hell, there are fourteen year old girls pregnant with their second child by their own choices. An infant doesn't understand consequences and choices and, if they can not understand choices, they can not be expected to make choices. Therefore, neither demons nor angels can talk to them."

"And since they can not be spoken to this way, the communication can not be intensified into possession?"

She took her cup in hand again. "Right."

He thought about it further. "So angels do not attempt possession because it is forbidden but they have the potential for it."

"Yes."

"Though the law wouldn't stop a fallen angel…or an angel that quit…like you."

Faith leaned back in her chair with a shrug.

"And it comes down to willpower…so if someone was in despair…or strung out…or hopeless…"

"It would be easier to take control. The less the mortal fights back, the easier."

He tilted his head as he continued to think. "In the bible…there's a story…a demon possession by legion but you say it's rare."

"Would you say that less than one in ten thousand is rare?"

Bruce nodded.

"There are more than ten thousand demons. Angels and demons do not equal you mortals in the billions but we are not numbered only in the thousands either. Legion was one hundred demons. There were more than a million demons even back then…and that man…he did not have the will to fight. You don't know what he had been through…what his life was like before legion. With the legion inside him, he was powerful. People were afraid of him. He could not be forced…and…" Her hands gripped tighter. "The were so terrified of him when legion came on him. He was stronger, tougher. No chains could hold him. No one could stand against him…hurt him."

Her voice had taken a softer, more reflective tone and Bruce attempted to mirror it with his own. "Did you know him?"

Faith nodded. "Yes. He was one of mine. I failed him, just like I failed so many back then…failed him, failed her."

"Her?" He was careful to be gentle in his prodding, not wanting her to realize how much she was talking.

She nodded with a shuddering breath. "A little girl...a slave." She took a deeper breath and her voice turned bitter. "Slaves are not prized when they have any will of their own. And the demon helped her. At least she saw it that way. Through the possession, she was allowed to prophesy. She was earning her owners big bucks and they treated her like the cash cow she was. She got a better life than your average slave girl because they were protecting valuable property. She didn't really have a reason to fight. I could not find a reason for her to fight them, to accept my help to fight them." She looked up at him. "They were a blessing in her eyes and all I was, was a guardian angel that could defend her from a vampire but not starvation or the cold or a master's whip."

"But they were banished..."

She gave another short bark of laughter. "Yes, but not by an angel. Legion was banished by the Son of God Himself. You're talking a completely different power level there and the little girl was saved by a man God personally spoke to, converted. Paul spoke with the power of God in his words...something I could not do." She sighed. "You know, I still believed in you then...not now." Bruce sensed a change in her eyes, felt a dark chill in her gaze as it rested on him. "You know, He, like His Father, has faith in all of you. They're waiting for you to get off your collective asses and use that intelligence and will that you're all so proud of to do something about this shithole of a world you all created together."

Bruce ignored her comments about the world. He understood her view but he needed to concentrate on what he could fix, not what he wished. "And Jasper? His being a drug addict...his will would already be low."

Faith nodded and leaned forward again. "Do you really want to know if you let an evil monster go? If he's off even now beating someone or killing someone or raping someone?"

"Would you know?" Bruce eyed her suspiciously. "I didn't think you had any kind of remote viewing."

"I don't. But I saw his eyes, even possessed, I saw Jasper."

"Do you know why he did it?"

She nodded.

"How much do you know?"

Faith leaned in closer and he could feel her gaze boring into his. "Everything. I was able to see his eyes when you questioned him. Do you really want to know what you let loose in the world? Can you handle what dark evil things you might find out? That might show you what a mistake it was to release him?"

"Tell me. If I screwed up, I screwed up." Bruce leaned in closer, steeling himself for the story, knowing he probably wouldn't like it.

"He's the son of a prostitute. He was put on drugs by her and her pimp because he objected to being sold when he was younger. It made him more tractable. It's a common trick of pimps, particularly with the young, as I'm sure you know. He went to jail the first time when he was in his young teens because they forgot his fix and he saw the pimp beat his mother, trying to force her to have a miscarriage. He was bigger than the pimp and enraged. He grabbed a pipe and he beat the man nearly to death. He thought the asshole was dead but he didn't make sure. So, he went to jail and, suddenly, he has a warm place to sleep every night and he's fed three times every day and he's given some teaching. He's still being used by the other inmates and he's still hooked on the drugs…but he's warm and he's fed. Then, he's released. He's free but he doesn't know any other way to make a living. So, it's back to the streets and the drugs. He doesn't hurt people for money but he does hurt people. He sees a john slap around a little thirteen year old hooker. He rams the guy into a wall, repeatedly, never feeling his own knuckles break on the guy's face because he's high. The man does not press charges because of the underage girl. He's been in plenty of fights always with pimps and johns…anyone he thinks is mistreating the hookers on the streets. Besides, he likes jail. He eats better and lives better in jail than he does on the streets. To go to jail for murder, well that's a guaranteed good life for him. Even better, he goes in as a terrifying insane serial killer, he gets to go into maximum security, maybe even solitary. Then not even the other inmates can bother him. Sounds like heaven. At least to someone who goes through life being used by anyone with a couple of bucks that will be just enough for the drugs needed to ignore that he's sleeping on the streets, hungry and cold."

As she leaned back, finished, Bruce thought about what she had said. He had been right. He didn't like the story. However, it did make him happier to know that he hadn't released a killer onto the streets. Then another thought occurred to him. "So, he still hopes to improve his life? Even if through jail?"

She nodded in agreement. "Even after everything he's been through, everything he's seen, he still has faith."

He studied her for a few moments. "Maybe you should take a lesson from him."

Her laugh was derisive and grating. "You're judging me? Comparing him and me? He's kept his faith, hope, for less than three decades. I kept mine for more than three thousand years." Her voice lowered into a hiss as she leaned forward again. "I kept it through that cursed city of child burning. I remained faithful through the massacres of Rome and the witch burning Inquisition. I did my work as best I could when the so called Crusades descended on villages and committed atrocities that would impress demons all in the name of God whom they betrayed. The concentrations camps, the rape of Nanking, the child soldiers of Africa. Through all the long centuries, I kept my faith. I did my job. Fought for you mortals, bled for you, cried for you as I begged my charges to do what was right, to show one ounce of compassion in this hell begotten world. Over three thousand years of this shit and you dare sit there and judge me?"

Bruce leaned into her, not backing down. "Maybe, Maybe not. But there's a difference you're not admitting. It wasn't happening to you. You could go to heaven and ask God why this was going on, take a break, get help. He's been in the middle of this shit with no way out, no place to rest and no one to explain why to him. And it may have only been going on for him for twenty-something years but that's his whole life, not the blink of an eye like it is to you. So, yeah, he got himself possessed but you say he hasn't given up and I think, maybe, you should look at that."

For once she had no come back but he could feel the rage radiating off of her as she turned her head away from him and finished her coffee.

CHAPTER TWENTY

The coffee was long since gone. Deciding they had spent enough time sitting in silence, he opened his mouth to suggest they leave. Suddenly, Faith sat up straight, her head tilted to the side as if listening.

A tense, "Bastards!" escaped her lips as she lunged out of her chair, vaulting the low wall of the patio in an easy movement that flowed into a ground eating sprint headed straight for the tree line.

Bruce was after her an instant later, not sure what had set her off but determined to keep her in sight. His longer legs closed the gap between them as she dodged in among the trees, and he easily followed the dark blue of her sweatshirt as she crashed through the brush, making no effort at stealth.

He arrived in a small hidden clearing moments behind her, just in time to see her grab a man by his neck and arm and bodily lift him from the ground and hurl him at least four feet into a thick oak. Bruce's mind quickly took in the scene of the woman in the dirt, blood oozing from her nose and a split lip, clothes shredded across the ground even as Faith sent a front kick into the face of a second man who had been holding the woman's wrists down. The force of it sent the target reeling back, crimson spraying from an obviously broken nose.

Bruce moved forward, hand on his gun but the angel warned him off with a sharp glance, quickly stripping off her sweatshirt and throwing it at him. "Deal with her. I've got these."

He noticed the back of her shirt was already charred as Faith turned to the first man who was pushing himself up to his feet, one hand scrambling to hold up his unfastened pants while brandishing a knife with the other.

"You don't know who you fuckin' with, bitch."

Faith moved forward, grey eyes cold. "Oh, yes I do. Jeremy." In a blur of motion, she caught the thug's arm and bent it with an audible crack.

Bruce was already stripping off his own coat as he knelt beside the bleeding woman, speaking softly and reassuringly to her while keeping an eye on the situation as a whole, just in case.

The angel lifted her opponent off his feet again, this time easily hurling him into his companion who had just risen with a gun and a string of profanities. They both fell to the ground in a crash and even angrier curses and Faith was on them before they could untangle themselves. The action was hard to follow in the close melee of bodies but Bruce did distinguish the sounds of more bones breaking followed by a scream of, "My hand! You goddamned bi—". Then the voice was cut off and a gun went flying to the other side of the clearing. A high pitched squeal while he was helping the victim into his coat told Bruce one of the men probably had gotten a sneaker shod foot to the groin. Usually he would have winced in sympathy but, in this case, all he felt was a grim approval.

Helping the woman over to a tree she could sit against somewhat comfortably while awaiting medical care, he reached into his coat for a phone. However, he paused as the woman's good eye widened and her jaw went slack in an expression of either awe or terror, he wasn't sure which.

With a muttered, "What now?" he turned and instantly understood.

Faith's wings blazed brightly in the shadowed clearing as the two criminals cowered before her, cradling broken limbs to their chests. "How dare you!" The angel's voice was resonant with her fury. "How dare you attack another, you parasites? Bad enough you've destroyed your own lives but to spread it…I should rip those cold dead hearts out of your chests and do the world a favor."

From somewhere deep, one found the courage or desperation to argue back for his life. "You don' know—don't understand how hard—"

"I understand, Jeremy, how you wasted your talent and opportunities to come to this."

The other seemed inspired by his friend or her willingness to respond without more physical violence. "What fuckin' opportunities? We was born with nothin'."

Faith lifted her hand and they cowered again. "Nothing? You were born with free will, talent. You, Jeremy, had a talent of colors, shapes. You could have easily been a master of painting but you use those gifted fingers to rob, hurt. You, Patrick, your talent with numbers that makes money with the bookies, that remembers bribe amounts, drug cutting quantities, could have been used as a leading scientist. But you wasted it all. You chose to be nothing but vermin that should be exterminated."

"Choices?" Patrick found his voice again, though it was shaking with fear of the flame winged woman looming over him. "What choice I got? You don' know shit 'bout where I'm from. Ain't no way out of the projects? Nothin' but take it or lose it."

Bruce could imagine the sneer on her face to match her voice. "And who makes it that way?"

"The rich folks, the politicians and them thug cops…like that one behind you. They make it bad for all of us."

"Really? Which cop forced you to steal your grandmother's checks, Jeremy? Which politician made her miss her heart medications so you could party with your friends, which one told you that your beer was more important than her health? Which rich man forced your hand to beat up a thirteen year old for looking at you 'the wrong way', big man? And you, Patrick, when did this cop force you to beat your woman so badly that you murdered your own child? How exactly did any politician force you to take your mother's bill money for a new gold chain causing the heat to be turned off? When did the rich people wander your neighborhoods and force you to break windows and trash parks? Tell me which policeman forced either of you to not pay attention at school, to not even try to learn. You did it to yourselves but you'll not do it to another." Her voice dropped into an arctic temperature as she reached down inhumanly fast and grabbed their throats in each hand, fingers closing and crushing as she lifted them from the ground.

She meant to do it. Bruce had no doubt about it. She meant to kill them and he couldn't let her.

Drawing his gun, he quickly moved across the small clearing and placed the muzzle at the base of her skull, licking his lips nervously as the heat of her wings washed over his bare face. "Let them go."

"I will when they've been made harmless."

"Let them go, Faith. Now." He could hear choking and lessening struggles. There wasn't much time. "I told you no killing. I'm not a liar and I swear, I'll shoot you right now if you don't stop."

Two bodies hit the ground, limp.

Faith looked over her shoulder, staring at him with her grey eyes. "You would have pulled the trigger…for them." It was not a question but he answered anyway.

"Yes. No more murders that I can stop."

Her head tilted slightly. "Do you think they'd be worth it? Losing what small aid I've been to your case?"

Bruce's voice remained steady and strong. "The ends don't justify the means."

She smirked at him. "Fine, I won't kill them today. Have you summoned aid for her yet?"

Bruce shook his head slightly. "About to." He put his gun away and moved around Faith to secure the two men before calling in for back up and medical care, giving his position as best he could. The two men were breathing but they had deep bruises on their necks. He wasn't that sympathetic but his mind began working on how he was going to explain all of this as he moved back towards the woman to check on her again.

"You should have let her kill them." Her voice was full of hatred and anger and Bruce could understand her point of view.

However, "She can't be judge, jury and executioner. No one has the right to be all three. But they'll go to jail for a long time."

The woman snorted in disbelief. "Yeah, if they don't get off for insanity or I don't get carted off for it. The burning wings are not going to go over well you know."

Bruce nodded in understanding. He was going to have a lot of explaining to do and he wasn't sure how he was going to do that...maybe the sun glinting off metal gave the illusion of wings, maybe just claim the guys were on drugs...but that might require a test to prove it. He glanced over at Faith and saw her crouching between the two prisoners, leaning in and speaking quietly, her wings still flaring brightly. Then, suddenly, the air seemed to fold or shimmer, he wasn't sure how to explain it, but in a second, she was gone.

The two young men looked pale as death, eyes wide in horror. Bruce wondered what she had done but was quickly distracted by the sound of sirens approaching.

CHAPTER TWENTY-ONE

The arrest and processing of the thugs went much easier than Bruce could have anticipated. The two men did not confess but whatever Faith had said to them was keeping them silent. There were not even the usual jeers and insults that often accompanied most any arrest, just sullen silence as rights were read and they were loaded into ambulances.

Bruce didn't bother to worry about what she had said further, just accepted it and let it go. The victim went along with the story that a concerned citizen had appeared on the scene before Bruce, fleeing before the detective arrived on the scene, afraid of being arrested for assault. This served the dual purpose of excusing Bruce from the charges of misconduct and explaining the various wounds on the culprits.

Her version did draw out some sarcasm from one of the officers that heard her report. "What is this? A comic book? Some guy with their underwear on the wrong side of their pants flies in, beats the shit out of two gang members and disappears? I guess he was too fast for you to get a good look at him too, huh? Or was he wearing a mask?"

Bruce had been about to put him in his place but the victim retaliated first, glaring at the man. "I never said I didn't get a good look at my savior. I got a real good look. I'll know them if I ever see them again and I'll offer them a steak dinner or the shirt off my back or anything they ask. But if you think I'll give you one bit of help to catch them, you're crazy."

The lieutenant had been there and had stared sternly at the sarcastic officer, cowing the young man from responding to the woman's challenging tone. Satisfied, he had turned a more sympathetic face to the victim. "Ma'am, I know you've been through hell today but this guy is guilty of assault. I'm not going to say those two didn't deserve it, however—"

She cut him off harshly. "However, nothing. I don't care if they're permanently maimed. I'll help you put them in jail but I think the world would be a better place if they were dead. There's no way I was their first victim and I believe they deserve every broken bone and they're getting off lightly." The last was said with her eyes on Bruce and he really couldn't find it in his heart to blame her.

Apparently, the lieutenant saw it as a lost cause. "Yes, ma'am. I understand. The EMTs want to take you to Martin Luther Memorial for an exam and to gather any physical evidence for the trial."

She nodded then glanced at Bruce again. "I'd like to talk to him for a moment before I go."

There was no reason to object. The lieutenant and the EMTs moved away to give them some privacy, obviously assuming she just wanted to thank him. Bruce wasn't so sure that's why she wanted to talk and let her speak first.

"I'm not crazy, am I? That was an angel...a real one? Not some bullshit special effects trick?"

Bruce considered lying but what would be the point? "Yes, she's a real angel. It wasn't a hallucination or trick of the light."

"Is she your guardian angel?"

"For the moment." Her eyes narrowed and Bruce realized how flippant the answer had sounded. He tried to explain. "She's working with me right now. Guardian angels have a lot of assignments and work."

She nodded in understanding. "Yeah, like cops do. This world is really going to hell." She smiled softly and Bruce saw a seed of wonder in her eyes. "But angels do exist."

"Yes." He didn't see any reason to crush the small light. "They exist."

She was quiet for a few more moments then refocused on him. "Stupid question...do they eat?" Her half smile showed slight embarrassment and apology.

Bruce hesitated, quickly deciding what part of the truth to tell her and what was just too complicated to get into. "They can and do."

She blushed a bit deeper but spoke anyway. "I'm the manager at Tony's over on Ninth. Stop by some time and I'll treat you both to whatever you want on the menu." She turned towards the waiting ambulance but paused and looked back at him. "You think I have a guardian angel?"

Bruce gave her a reassuring smile. "Didn't that just get proven today? Just don't go wandering down dark alleys and making more work for her, ok?" It wasn't the full truth, he knew. She had to have a guardian angel, Faith said everyone did, but it definitely wasn't Faith. Still, Bruce saw no reason to be brutally honest. The woman had been through enough trauma without him stomping on her comforting thoughts.

As the ambulance pulled away, Lieutenant Spyden approached Bruce. "Well?"

"Well what?"

"How did you get mixed up in all of this?" The man crossed his arms, studying Bruce closely.

The detective shrugged, trying to end this fast. He needed to figure out how to find Faith again. "You heard the report. I heard the screams and came looking."

"Uh-huh." The lieutenant watched him expectantly for several silent moments. "So, you want to tell me the rest?"

"The rest?" The confusion was not fully feigned.

"Yeah, like what you're doing in the park on duty? No murder cases out here and you don't do patrols." Bruce's mind raced. "Also, where's your shadow?"

"My shadow?" A calm expression wasn't easy to maintain under the circumstances but he thought he mostly managed it.

"I'm not deaf and Mary hasn't been too quiet about her distaste for the female vagrant you've had around lately...especially when others have been curious enough to ask about it."

Bruce groaned internally but quickly put together a plausible excuse. "She wandered off while I was working on the arrest. You know how they are." It was the easiest explanation and the closest to the truth.

Lieutenant Spyden stared hard at Bruce. "Don't treat me like an idiot. She's stuck around for more than a day and in a police sweatshirt that you're now holding. Why've you kept her around and what really happened here?"

Bruce furiously came up with and discarded things to say. He had no intention of telling the truth. He'd end up in a straight jacket. "She wasn't always staying close. I've had to go find her again several times. Lucky for me, she keeps eating at the same soup kitchen. I've been keeping her around because I have reason to believe the Saint T. Claus killer is hiding in the transient population and that she knows something about it."

"And you were down here....why?"

"Because there are rumors of people living in the park. I was hoping I could get her to lead me to likely spots and maybe help me talk to them when I heard the screams. She took off somewhere in the middle of it."

He could see Spyden mentally working through it. "And she left a warm intact piece of clothing behind?" The man glanced down significantly at the blue sweatshirt Faith had thrown at Bruce earlier.

He silently cursed himself for not giving it back before she had disappeared but he hadn't thought about it with her wings shining brightly. He'd had other things on his mind. "I...don't know." He just couldn't come up with anything better right now.

"Maybe she didn't like the lettering." Spyden held his gaze. He knew Bruce was hiding things. The detective was sure of that, could read it in his superior's eyes. "I've given you enough rope to hang yourself before, Bruce, but never this much and not with the FBI on my ass." The lieutenant paused again and the detective waited nervously. "Get me that killer."

"And the reports?"

"Don't get caught and don't fuck up the conviction." No more was said as Lieutenant Spyden returned to his car.

CHAPTER TWENTY-TWO

Bruce ran his hand through his short black hair as he sat in his car. He had looked all around the park and the vehicle, even up at the trees and telephone poles nearby but he had found no sign of Faith. Where could she have gone? Last time, she had shown up pretty much as soon as he was alone. However, last time, she had not had her wings out and had not just disappeared. She had been moving around a crime scene like any human.

He shook his head. No use reviewing the differences between now and then. He needed to focus on where she could be. Well, she kept talking about crawling back into the bottle as soon as this case was closed and she had just seen yet another example of the kind of wasted lives that had sent her there in the first place. Deciding it was the most likely option, he pulled out into the streets heading towards the darker side of town and the bar where he had first met her.

He was preoccupied enough that he almost forgot to check his glove box but the habit of being prepared saved him. The compartment was empty of chocolate bars so he pulled into a convenience store and replenished the supply before heading into the rundown area that was home to the shadow races. Pulling into the parking lot of the fast food restaurant turned bar where he had first met Faith, he stepped out of his car and called out his usual deal to the fair folk, tossing two of the candy bars into the shadows behind him as he strode across the overgrown cracked asphalt. He consciously ignored the black winged horse tethered in the deep shadows around the side of the building and, reaching under his jacket, he adjusted his sidearm and stepped in through the painted door.

It took him the usual few moments for his eyes to adjust to the dim smoky interior and he stepped to the side so he was no longer blocking the door while he searched for anyone familiar. He did not see multihued golden hair or flame wings or a slumped over cloaked figure anywhere. He did, however, see Tiver. It was a long shot that the wererat might know where Faith was since, as far as Bruce knew, wererats didn't travel planes like an angel apparently did. However, he could not think of a better option at the moment.

Walking over to the bar, he was careful to avoid the various beings at the tables. He did not need trouble tonight and he knew from past experience that humans were not exactly welcome here. Many shadow races had long lives and longer memories.

Stepping up next to the slim man, he leaned on the polished plastic counter. "Hey Tiver."

The wererat nodded back, his eyes flickering around the room nervously. "What do you want?"

"I'm looking for information on lost angels."

Tiver stared at him in surprise. "What?"

"Where would an angel hang out in the city if they don't want to be found?"

Black eyes glanced around again and the slim man leaned in closer to Bruce to keep the conversation private. "I told you before what I knew about where angels in the city are. I don't know anything about where your killer might be and I told you the one that was here wouldn't help you."

The human lowered his voice. "Actually, she's been helping me but she slipped off today and I'm trying to find her. I thought she might come back here."

"She hasn't. I haven't seen her since you carried her out of here."

Bruce thought for a few moments. "Do you know where else she might be? Where else she was prone to hang out?"

The slim man shook his head again. "No. A couple of month ago, she just showed up out of nowhere, sat down in that corner and ordered a drink. Never said anything else except ordering the drink, never left the corner until you came and pulled her out. No one knew where she came from. No one was brave enough to bother her after she took out a group of elf gang members that decided to be tough by knocking over her drink."

He considered the new bit of information. "Did she kill any of them?"

"No. But the healers had a problem putting them back together. She not only broke bones, she powdered a few. Far as I hear, a few of them are still going back to the healers."

Bruce nodded. He could believe considering he was pretty sure that one of the arms of the thugs today was never going to be the same again. It had been mangled almost beyond recognition when they had loaded him into the ambulance.

Tiver's eyes flicked behind him. "You better take off. Some of the natives are restless."

Bruce knew better than to ignore a warning from Tiver, so he threw a few bills down on the bar and was turning, ready to leave, when his way was blocked by three large males of indeterminate race since, currently at least, they appeared human. Bruce muttered an 'Oh hell' under his breath.

"We don't like your kind 'round here." The one in the middle spoke with an odd growl to his voice and Bruce was even less happy.

He had heard that growling accent before, werewolves and young ones at that. He judged their age at just old enough to either be breaking away from their parent's pack or getting ready to challenge for dominance, either way meant they were out to prove themselves. "I was just leaving." He casually reached back as if to scratch his back but, in reality, wrapped his hand around his pistol.

The large speaker smirked down at him. "Nah, since you like it so much in the shadows, we'll just make you a permanent resident."

Bruce tried to gauge the distance to the door. Regular bullets would not do any real harm to these three but the stopping power of the bullet might push them back enough to buy him the time to get out the door and to his car. He couldn't outrun them on foot but he could in a car. Even as he considered it, though, he knew he was fooling himself. The handgun was not powerful enough, the distance was too far and there were three of them. He, also, was not counting on help from any corner. No one here had reason to back him and risk retribution from these three so Tiver's voice startled him as much as it startled the wolves.

"Back off, guys, and let him leave."

The young leader turned his head and growled at the wererat but, with the other two continuing to focus on the human, Bruce still had no opportunity to try anything. "Stay out of this, scavenger, or become prey."

"Fuck you." Bruce had known Tiver was no coward but this seemed crazy to Bruce. "Look, boy, he comes here and he spends human money. The kind of money that your daddy borrowed off of me to get your momma the extra milk and calcium vitamins she needed when she was carrying last. So, Junior, your daddy owes me. Do you want me spending that favor having him come and remind you that you're not alpha of the pack yet?"

The large werewolf held Tiver's gaze, glaring, and Bruce was guessing that he was deciding if he was ready to challenge his father or not.

Suddenly, a third voice was heard from. "You know, I already put two little shits in the hospital today. It won't bother me to put you three there as well."

Bruce recognized the voice even before he glimpsed the blazing wings between the bodies as the werewolves turned.

They were brave. He would admit that. They did not run.

"This isn't your business. The human's on our territory. He brought it on himself. It's not unauthorized hunting."

Faith laughed her usual derisive laugh. "You have me confused with someone else. I don't answer to heaven or hell's rules. I don't give a shit about authority or lack of it. Now, get the fuck out or I'm going to start ripping parts off."

They were not cowards but they were, apparently, not going to argue with an angel over a human and a wererat. The three walked out the door without further word.

Faith watched them go then tuned to look at Bruce. "Since you brought me here, does this mean I can get a drink now?"

CHAPTER TWENTY-THREE

Bruce stared at her. "Where have you been?"

She smirked at him. "That's not a no." Stepping up to the bar, Faith looked at the slim dark haired elf. "Oblivion. Now."

The detective immediately turned to the bartender. "Don't give it to her." Returning his attention to Faith, he again demanded, "Where have you been?"

Faith leaned on the counter. "Where's my sweatshirt? Oh and you're welcome by the way."

Bruce remembered his manners while noticing the bartender ignoring his instructions and placing a glass of black inky fluid in front of Faith. She reached for it and Bruce took it out of her hand. "Thank you for the save. I do appreciate it." He tried to hand the glass back to the bartender. "I said no."

The bartender behind the counter backed away, shaking his head, his fine boned expression guarded, obviously unwilling to get involved.

Faith grabbed the drink back. "You better not have thrown that sweatshirt away after I tossed it to you for safekeeping." She raised the drink to her lips.

Bruce grabbed it and dumped it on the floor. "I told you no, and the sweatshirt is in the car."

Her wings rippled menacingly as she glared at him. "That was my drink."

"And that's my floor. Maybe you stop makin' trouble and go 'fore I make you go." The bartender had reentered the discussion at this point, his emerald elven eyes sparkling with annoyance and some nervousness as he toyed with a long rune decorated dagger.

It occurred to Bruce that getting into a fight as a human in a shadow world bar, the only one where he could get reliable supernatural information, was probably not his best idea. He gave the bartender his most apologetic look. "I'm sorry for the disturbance and your floor. Here's something for your trouble." He lay down several large bills on the counter then grabbed Faith's arm. "Let's go."

"I haven't had my drink."

"And you won't."

She smirked at him. "Oh really and how will you stop me?"

Bruce's mind raced. He could not physically force her but there were other ways. He stared her straight in the eye. "If we don't leave now then I'm going to sit here next to you until you pass out drunk. Then, I'll carry you out of here again. Only, this time, I'll dump you in the shower and turn on the cold water to wake you up."

Faith glared. "You're enough of a bastard to do it, too." Easily shaking free of his grip, she stalked out the door.

Bruce paused long enough to give Tiver some money and a hurried 'Thanks for the backup' before quickly leaving as well, ignoring the whispers that followed him out. As they emerged into the afternoon sun, her wings dissipated, leaving an unmarked back and a shirt gone from shoulder blades to waist with black charred edges that flaked off as she walked.

She waited as he opened the car and hit the button to unlock her side before tossing the other two candy bars into the bushes.

They were silent while he carefully maneuvered the car out of the shadow area of town and she pulled on the too big sweatshirt again.

"So, where were you?"

She answered with a question. "Where are we going?"

"Faith, where were you?"

He knew she was her rolling her eyes though she had pulled the hood up again. "You are so fucking annoying."

"Then answer me. You know I'll keep asking until you do."

He could hear her grind her teeth but she answered...sort of. "Where do you think I was? Use your brain for something other than pissing me off for once."

Bruce opened his mouth to retort but closed it again, considering her words and what he knew about her and angels in general. Thinking back to how she had disappeared, the answer came to him. "You shifted to another plane."

"Yeah the soul plane. Easiest for me to go to. Figured it'd scare them more too, afraid I might just appear from anywhere."

"So, then...what?" He thought again. "You couldn't just have headed to the bar...you said that plane gives no clues to physical areas except through your charges...and you gave up your charges. How did you get there?" His mind put together some pieces. "You were following me weren't you?"

"Yeah."

"So, I'm one of your charges." Something didn't seem right. "But you don't have any charges. You quit."

Faith laughed sardonically. "As usual, you're so close and you're completely wrong. You're not one of my charges. Like you said, I quit."

"Then explain it to me. How did you follow me if you don't have charges?"

"Where are we going?"

Bruce sighed. "We're heading to a soup kitchen. There's about three of them in the middle of the area covered by the murders. I'm hoping the killer might be working out of a central location. Now, how does this tracking work?"

"Angels only have to eat once a week. You told me it's been less than a week since the first killing. So, I don't think he or she is going to be a regular or even remembered." For once, her voice wasn't sarcastic but just confused. It was a definite change.

"Don't worry about it. I've got some ideas. Now how does the tracking work?"

He could hear her grinding her teeth. "Fine and I'll use small words for you too." That set his own teeth to grinding but he refused to retort, waiting for the promised explanation. "Once an angel has a…well, scent is probably the easiest description to use…anyway, once an angel has a scent of a being, we can follow it anywhere through the soul plane."

"And how do you get this scent?"

"With mortals and followers, we just have to read them. From the first time I read a person's eyes, I can remember it and I can find them. I've read you. I can follow you anywhere at anytime." He saw her turn to him out of the corner of his eye. "Does that scare you? That even after you're done with me, you can't escape me if I'm not done with you?"

He ignored her question and kept his eyes on the road and away from hers. "So, why didn't you show up earlier? I went to the bar looking for you. Why did you make me waste the time and not just show up when I got into the car?"

She sighed. "I didn't know you were in the car. I've told you, from the soul plane, I can't read your environment. I can only read you. I didn't want to just appear in front of a bunch of mortals. After I'd just gone out of my way not to have to explain my wings, I was not just going to leap out in front of a bunch of your buddies. I was waiting until you were calm. Figured once you weren't nervous, it would be safe to come back, that you'd be in your apartment or something like that but you never did calm down. So, I just waited. Then you got scared and felt in danger and I decided it was time I showed up."

He smiled, even laughed a little.

Her voice turned suspicious. "What's so funny?"

"Looks like I got my own guardian angel watching over me now, huh?"

"'Course you do." She paused and let him enjoy the thought of an angel watching his back for a moment. "Because once this is done, I'm going to pay you back for all the memories you've made me relive and all the time you've kept me away from forgetting. Until I get my pound of flesh, no one else gets to kill you."

He wasn't sure if she was joking or not but he no longer felt reassured about her being able to find him anywhere.

CHAPTER TWENTY-FOUR

They were at the second of the three soup kitchens on Bruce's list and Faith was pouting behind him. Pouting wasn't a word Bruce would use to describe her within her hearing but it was definitely an accurate description. She was leaning on the wall in sullen silence. Her head was down and her hands were shoved into the pocket of her hooded sweatshirt. All in all, her attitude was not making his questioning of the staff any easier.

They had already offered her a meal and clothes which she had rejected with a growled, "Don't worry about it, he's feeding me and gave me warm clothes. Save them for the real needy."

That had earned him some very strange looks and a pointed question from the supervisor, Linda Mallard, whom he'd just introduced himself to.

"So, you are taking this young woman under your protection?"

He immediately understood the subtle implications of what she was asking. It was not that unheard of for unsavory people to grab up a homeless person with promises of food and clothing only to abuse them in some way. "No. She's helping me on one of my cases in exchange for new clothes and meals while she works with me. All she does is provide me with information."

Linda did not seem convinced. "Does she know that she can leave at any time?"

Bruce cleared his throat and swallowed down both a laugh and a sarcastic comment. "Yes, she definitely knows."

Behind him, Faith was not so kind. "If I truly decide to fucking leave, he wouldn't be able to stop me. I'm not a charity case, I'm a hard case so could you just leave me the hell alone now."

Bruce groaned as the charity worker's face hardened and he tried his friendliest smile. "As you can see, she's not downtrodden. So, back to my original questions...I'm investigating a string of murders in the city and I have reason to suspect that it might be the work of a transient. I was wondering if you could tell me if someone new has shown up lately."

She gave him a look then stated the obvious. "We always have a changing sea of faces here. New ones show up every day and old ones disappear just as quickly. We try to help them find a way to transition out of this lifestyle but, as I'm sure your companion can tell you, this is difficult at best."

The detective nodded. "I understand that. This one, however, might be a bit more noticeable. He or she would probably only have shown up once or twice so far and would have kept his or her eyes or upper face shielded or shadowed at all times."

Linda looked past him for a moment. "Like her?"

Bruce glanced over his shoulder at Faith before turning back to Linda. "Yes, like her. That's why she's helping me on this."

"Well, there is one. He showed up a few days ago and then again tonight. Doesn't talk, refused everything except one plate of food and sat in a corner away from everyone."

"Tonight? How long ago did he leave?"

"Well…I think he's still…" She trailed off as she looked around and frowned. "That's funny. He was right over there when you walked in and I don't remember him leaving."

Bruce looked in the direction she was facing and noticed an empty table in the corner with an almost empty tray sitting on it. He began looking around quickly, his hand reaching back for his pistol out of habit. There was no one with a hood pulled down or dark glasses.

He could hear Linda asking the other volunteers if they had seen the man leave but he was pretty sure they had not. If it was his real quarry, he knew the man could have disappeared within a second. Instead of focusing on where he was now, he asked Linda if she could provide more information about him.

"Our files are confidential."

It was not an unexpected answer but it was very frustrating. "Look, I'm not trying to persecute anyone and I'm not just trying to find anyone to pin this on. If he's innocent, then I'll be happy to buy him hot meals for a week to make up for any inconvenience of being brought in for questioning. However, if he's guilty, I need to stop him. I don't want to cause you or anyone here any problems but people are out there dying and they are going to keep dying if I can't catch the right person. So, please, tell me everything you can about him so that I can find him. If he's the wrong person, fine, I'll give him money, I'll feed him, whatever to make it right and, then, I can focus on finding the right person…but if it is him, the sooner I get him off the streets, the safer it will be. Please, just forget the red tape and the procedures and just help me out here."

Linda stared hard at him for several moments after he was done with his plea, considering, and then said, "Wait here."

He nodded but did not completely obey, grabbing Faith's arm as he walked over to where the person had been sitting. Waiting a few moments, he looked at her expectantly. "Well?"

She stared back at him calmly. "Well what?"

"Was the killer here?"

Her voice dripped disdain. "And I'm supposed to know this, how?"

Bruce gritted his teeth. "Ok, ok. So you can't know for sure if the guy here was the killer but was he an angel?"

"Why do you think I would know?"

Bruce closed his eyes and quickly counted to ten before glaring at her. "Because you have senses beyond a human. You knew Jasper was possessed by a demon. You heard the woman being attacked from across a park. You can read souls in people's eyes. So, was the guy here an angel or not."

She smirked and he ground his teeth. "None of those would help here, Billy boy."

"Why not?"

Her smirk grew. "I knew Jasper was possessed because I could see the demon in his eyes, same as reading any other soul. I heard the woman across the park because I have better hearing and sight and such than you do. His eyes aren't here for me to look at now are they?"

His mind worked for several minutes. "If you have better sight and hearing, wouldn't all five senses be better than human? Including scent?"

Her voice dripped disgust. "Do you think I'm going to sniff at this bench like some bloodhound after a runaway?"

Bruce opened his mouth but Linda was approaching with a few papers in hand and he let the matter drop.

She didn't mention that he had left the spot she'd told him to stay at but assumed that she was smart enough to realize he would want to investigate where the man had been sitting. "Here is everything we have on him. It's not much and I don't know how accurate it is. It's not unusual for people to lie about their names and such." She stared at Bruce hard. "Look, I care about people. I wouldn't be doing this otherwise and the only reason I'm giving you this is to try to help you stop a murderer. If I find out that you use this for any other reason or if this comes back on me or this place in any way, I will deny that I ever gave this to you and place charges of breaking and entering and burglary against you. You might get out of the charges but I will make enough of a stink to get your badge taken away just to shut me up. Understand?"

The detective nodded. "All I want is to stop a murderer. That's it."

He looked over at Faith. "Come on, we're leaving."

The angel stood staring into space for a few moments, probably just to punish him for the earlier conversation then turned and smirked. "Well, let's go then."

Bruce sighed and bit back another sarcastic comment before telling Linda goodbye and leading Faith out of the building.

CHAPTER TWENTY-FIVE

Bruce woke up to darkness and tried to figure out what had disturbed his sleep. He thought back over the night.

It had been a quiet evening though frustrating. He had come home to have dinner and think. Checking his email, he'd found nothing but spam. He was happy that the FBI agents were, apparently, not going to be breathing down his neck but he was disappointed not to have heard anything from Mary. Usually, she would have sent a reminder to let her know he was ok but not anymore it seemed.

He had sat down and gone over the file he had received on the transient he believed was the killer. There was not much. His name was Sam Night. Showing the name to Faith, he had asked if it meant anything to her.

She had shaken her head. "I've never heard of a Sam Night."

"Never?"

Faith shrugged. "The name means nothing to me."

Bruce had run the name through the computer, searching both the net and databases, but had come up with nothing as well. Of course, most soup kitchens did not put their file names in searchable databases. He had spent several minutes thinking about calling the kitchens in the last town that Saint T. Claus had hit but decided it would be a waste of time. Going through the rest of the file had been just as useless. Mr. Night refused any offers of sleeping in a shelter, had only shown up twice and Bruce highly doubted he would show up a third time, not after his disappearing act today.

The detective had double checked with dispatch before bed to make sure that the Saint T. Claus killer had not struck again without him being notified but the city was oddly quiet. There had been no new murders at all reported. So, not sure what else to do, he had gotten ready for bed, hoping his mind would come up with some way to track this Sam Night down if he got some sleep. Faith had been agreeable to the plan as well, muttering that he was easier to deal with when he was asleep as she lay down on the opposite edge of the bed, not even kicking off her shoes.

And now, here he was, awake in the middle of the night and not sure why.

Carefully rolling over and sitting up, he noticed that Faith was nowhere in the room despite it being around 1 am. He did not panic immediately. She'd already proven time and again that she was sticking around until the end for her own reasons. He wasn't exactly sure what those reasons were but he was sure she had some. That did not answer what had awoken him though he assumed it might be Faith if she had gotten up to make herself a sandwich or something.

He cocked his head to the side and listened. For a few moments, he heard nothing, no one moving through the apartment, no drawers or cabinets opening or closing. Then, he heard Faith's voice, muffled, and she did not sound happy. Cutting across her voice was another voice. That did not make Bruce happy. He stood up and quietly slid his pistol out of the holster next to the bed. He padded carefully across the room and slowly turned the handle, cracking open the door. Standing still, he listened for several moments trying to place the location of Faith and who or whatever the other voice was, hoping it was the TV.

It wasn't. Peering through the crack in the door, he saw down the short hallway that the living room was in complete darkness, no flickering light from the set and both voices sounded farther away.

Carefully slipping out of the bedroom, he took the few steps to the end of the hall and stood with his back pressed against the wall. The voices were clearer now though he still couldn't distinguish the individual words. Whoever she was speaking to was male and neither of them was happy.

He took a firmer grip on the pistol and cautiously peered around the corner.

Faith was out on the balcony and crouching on the railing, one hand holding the iron bar for balance, was a man. Bruce didn't recognize him though that didn't mean much. He was covered up like Faith usually was, a too-large hooded sweatshirt with the hood pulled low over his face, a heavy vest, gloves, heavy boots and well worn jeans.

Faith shook her head to whatever the man had just said, her voice becoming a little louder and more intense. He answered the same, his words and manner forceful but Bruce still couldn't understand the conversation. Whatever language they were speaking, it wasn't English. Though, as he listened, he finally thought he recognized it. It sounded like what she had sung the other night.

He was trying to decide whether to interrupt her conversation with what he assumed was another angel or not when they ended it suddenly.

The male struck the bar with a closed fist, his voice demanding. Faith apparently refused whatever he said because he turned and jumped down out of sight. Faith's head was lowered as she stepped back into the apartment, closing the door behind her and locking it before running her hand through her hair.

Bruce lowered the gun and stepped out into the living room. "Who was your friend?"

CHAPTER TWENTY-SIX

Faith lifted her head and glared at him challengingly, "Eavesdropping?"

Bruce shrugged. "Not really. I couldn't understand what either of you were saying."

"So why didn't you just fucking let me know you were listening?" Her voice sounded unusually strained, not as focused or angry as in previous conversations.

"Because I didn't know what was going on and I'm not stupid enough to crash in on two angels especially when I don't know one of them. You may not be ready to kill me but I'm pretty sure that doesn't go for everyone." They stared at each other in silence for several moments. "So, who was he?"

"Why do you think he was an angel?"

Bruce sighed. They had gone back to question for a question but he felt that it would not hurt to answer. "Because the language you were using sounded like that song you sang. I've never heard anything like that language from anyone else. So, I'm assuming it's an angel thing. He was also perched up on the rail, perfectly comfortable, unafraid of losing his balance. I don't think he came in through the door, especially as he dropped down without a problem, and we're not on the first floor and that's concrete down there not grass. All things you would do without a problem with but mortals wouldn't. So, who was he?"

Faith continued to stare at him, emotions passing quickly over her face, too fast for him to accurately read but she was not her usual angry self.

He decided to try another tact as the silence stretched. "So, did you switch to the strange language because you knew I was listening?"

She gave a short laugh. "I didn't know you were listening."

Bruce stared hard at her. "Bullshit, with your hearing—"

"What about my hearing?"

"If you can hear someone scream across the park, you can hear someone moving around this small of an apartment."

She crossed her arms over her sweatshirt covered chest, never having even removed her shoes before sleep. "Yeah...if I'm paying attention, I can hear a lot of things. Thing is, you are not the center of my universe. I don't stand around breathlessly listening for every little sound you make." Her voice dripped with mockery and Bruce gritted his teeth.

"I never said you did. I had just assumed—"

"And what do they say about assuming?" She cut him off again and Bruce was beginning to wonder at that. It was unusual for her.

So he resisted rising to the bait and thought about things. The tones of the voices had not been friendly, almost arguing. If she had been focused on the argument, it was not beyond belief that she had missed what he had been doing and, as far as he knew, she had not actually lied to him before. Misled, misdirected, allowed assumptions, gave opinions, yes, but never an actual lie. "So who was he?"

She glared at him and stepped further into the apartment.

Bruce waited, staring hard at her but she strode across the carpet without a word, brushing past him as she turned into the short hallway then turned again almost immediately into the bedroom. He followed her in, carefully holstering his pistol as she flopped down on the other side of the bed, putting her dirty shoes back up on the mattress, her back to him.

"Who is he?"

She still did not answer and her silence was beginning to unnerve him. Even when she had refused to answer before, she had always been very vocal about it. He sat down on the edge closer to the door, sure that she would not want him too near her.

"Faith, who is he?"

She still did not move but he was pretty sure she was not asleep. Her body was tense though her eyes were closed.

He reached out a cautious hand and shook her shoulder anyway, deciding to go ahead with the ploy. "Wake up, Faith. I'm not going to let you go to sleep until you tell me who he is."

Her voice was tight and stressed as she jerked her shoulder out of his grip. "Fuck off, Bruce. It won't work this time. So, shut up and go to sleep. No more answers tonight."

He blinked in surprise. This was the first time she had used his preferred nickname or this tone of voice. Deciding to leave it, he lay down on his side of the bed and closed his eyes, letting his mind work in the background as he slipped into dreams.

CHAPTER TWENTY-SEVEN

Bruce woke up to the smell of coffee and toast once again and he hoped it was a sign that Faith was over whatever had bothered her the previous night. Getting up, he gathered new clothes and crossed the hallway to the bathroom, getting ready for work quickly, mind already working on what to do that day. He needed to check his email and dispatch and dropping by the fibbie's commandeered office might not be a bad idea, see if they picked up anything else. He had found the soup kitchen he believed the killer had eaten at but it occurred to him that he didn't know how many angels like Faith were in the city. It was better to be thorough so a visit to the third soup kitchen on his list was also in order. Then he could start looking around at the area for possible places for the killer to be sleeping.

Dumping his clothes in the laundry basket, he headed out through the living room to the kitchen, grabbing some toast and coffee before sitting down on the couch.

Faith was sitting on the other end, staring off into space, her head cocked to the side as if listening but the television was off and all the windows were closed.

Bruce finished the toast and decided to try to find out her mood before starting on his schedule. "Hear anything interesting?"

She glanced over at him. "No. Just kids talking back to parents, a wife cheating on her husband, a boy bragging that he's about to be a father for the third time and is dodging child support payments again. The usual human conversations."

He took a sip of the hot coffee. "How good is your hearing? I mean, what is it like being able to hear all of that?"

Faith looked over at him, eyes narrowed suspiciously but her voice was calm when she answered. "I don't know what it's like not to be able to. However, if you're really wanting a description…and you always seem to…Think of it like a radio with scan on. Usually, it's just a lot of constant noise from all over because I can hear so much over a very long distance but, when you decide on a channel, it tunes in. It all depends on how much I focus and on what."

It was tempting to ask her again about the angel from last night but he hesitated. She was being agreeable but the look in her eyes told him she was still wary, not easy to trick or lead into an answer. "Ok, we have a full schedule ahead of us. Let's go."

She rolled her eyes as she pulled the hood up over her head. "Oh joy, can't wait."

Bruce decided to hit the soup kitchen first, before the rush, and it had been as empty of leads as the first soup kitchen. No sign of anyone that could have been a newly arrived angel.

Next, he went to the precinct house to check his email and dispatch. Sitting down, he nodded a greeting to Mary while Faith slumped into the chair next to his desk.

Mary nodded back. "Anything new?"

He shrugged. "Maybe." He brought up his computer, tapping in his passwords as he checked the dispatch notes of the previous night as well as his email address, nothing as of yet.

Mary leaned forward. "You know there are other murders out there to solve, right? I mean why not let the FBI handle this one."

Bruce turned towards her, suddenly suspicious. "Why the sudden hurry to drop this, Mary? I told you I'd give you all the credit."

She licked her lips and glanced over at Faith but the angel's head was down and her breathing was even as if asleep. Mary lowered her voice anyway. "Because, the more I think about this case, the more I know it's poison. This case brought that piece of trash into our lives and it's caused a rift between us that I don't like. Before all this, you trusted me and didn't treat me like the enemy. This thing is jinxed, Bruce, let's just drop it and go back to how it was before."

Bruce leaned in and lowered his voice as well, though not to prevent Faith from hearing, he was pretty sure she was actually awake. He just did not want the rest of the department listening in. This place was enough of a rumor mill as it was. "Look, Mary, maybe you're right and this case is jinxed, I don't know. But dropping it is not going to fix anything. I can't just magically forget the things you've done."

"I've done?" Her voice remained low in volume but rose in tone, expressing outrage. "You mean you believe her lie about me and the chief's wife?"

"I really don't care if you are or not, though if you are, it's not your best decision. However, you intentionally tried to railroad a man into jail just to get some fleeting glory and you almost sabotaged the case twice. Once with Jasper and then when you gave up all the files. If I hadn't made my own backups in the computer…" He shook his head a bit and got back on topic. "Look, Mary, I'm really not happy with what's happened. You're my partner and you've had my back more times than I can count but, right now, I don't know what to think of you and dropping this case is not going to change that." Her eyes flashed over to Faith and she opened her mouth to say something but Bruce cut her off first. "And don't you dare blame anyone other than yourself. You chose to try to screw me over by handing over the files; you chose to just railroad Jasper without a second thought, without any investigation. That was you and no one else. So if you don't like what's happened, that's your own problem and you'll have to fix it. And if you think it can't be fixed, then get a new partner."

She looked as if he had slapped her and he desperately wanted to take back the last words. He had not meant to say that, had let frustration, resentment and disappointment in her get the better of him. However, it was said now and it could not be unsaid, just as what she had done could not be undone.

Mary stood up without another word and stalked off down the hall.

Taking a deep breath, Bruce turned back to his computer, refusing to look over at Faith to see if she had been paying attention to their conversation.

About an hour later, he had a new map in his pocket marked with the known usual sleeping places of the homeless in the area and he powered down his computer as he stood up. "Faith." She looked up, her eyes shadowed but her mouth expressionless. "I'm going to go check with the FBI. Wait for me here, please."

If she was surprised by the politeness of his request, she gave no sign as she shrugged and lowered her chin to her chest again.

CHAPTER TWENTY-EIGHT

Agent Ferrous' eyes were not welcoming as Bruce stepped into the room but the detective hadn't expected any better.

"Have you brought any more information?" The fibbie started without any greeting.

Bruce almost shook his head but paused. They would know he had been out almost all yesterday and they would probably know about Jasper and the thugs at the park by now. However, they could not possibly guess at the full strangeness behind the events and it would be better to give them the mundane information rather than give them room to wonder and guess. "I checked out some soup kitchens in the area. Asked about new faces."

The other man's stony gaze did not waver. "You think all of this was done by a transient?" His voice was monotone enough that Bruce wasn't sure what the agent thought of the theory.

So, he gave a nod as his only answer.

Ferrous smirked. "Is that really your theory? Or is it just an excuse for that piece of tail you've been dragging around and enjoying on the tax payer's money? Having a little fun under the witness protection excuse?"

Bruce could have bristled at the accusation but it was such a ridiculously obvious ploy, he laughed instead, particularly at the thought of Faith as a 'piece of tail'.

The agent was not pleased with the response and his gaze burned with anger.

However, the detective simply smiled. "You're fishing with no bait. Even if there was anything inappropriate there, which there's not, I haven't used one cent from anywhere except my own pocket. So, it wouldn't be anyone's business except vice and, if you actually bring them in to accuse that woman of prostitution, they'll hurt themselves laughing."

"So what is she?" Ferrous's voice dropped from unfriendly to arctic.

"An expert on transience."

The agent's eyes narrowed in annoyance and it was obvious that he was trying to decide if Bruce was joking or not.

The detective almost sighed. This sparring was getting him nowhere but further on the fibbie's bad side. "Look, I believe this killer is part of the transient population but I don't know the ins and outs of that culture, lifestyle…whatever you want to call it. The woman out there, she does know it. So, she tells me how people like her survive and I get possible leads on tracking the guy down." He paused and crossed his arms, even as his eyes roamed the maps and papers tacked to the walls. "So, I told you what I've got. What've you found?"

Ferrous sneered. "You've got nothing."

Bruce shrugged. "I've got a workable theory, probably more than what you have." He moved closer to one of the walls, his mind quickly putting what he was reading together. "We're all on the same side here. We all want this guy stopped. I don't care about jurisdiction; I just care about stopping the bad guy."

Ferrous continued to glare at him for several moments as the detective continued to study the items pinned up on the wall. Finally, he growled out, "Just to get you out of the way, your theory's completely wrong."

Bruce looked back at him. "Oh?" He nodded toward one of the articles on the wall. "So you really think this is a cult thing?"

The agent gave the kind of long suffering sigh that Bruce usually received when someone recognized he was going to be more stubborn than them. "Whoever is doing this is too controlled to be a transient. The person doing the cutting is definitely skilled and educated and had access to a good amount of money to get the kind of quality blade necessary to make those cuts. They also know how to clean a crime scene perfectly which means a degree of education that would be able to gain employment. The mutilations and the writing on the wall are classic cult markings. The strength used in parts of the murders as well as the ability to deal with multiple people at the same time indicates more than one person involved."

The detective nodded as he returned to looking at the papers on the wall. "So you think it's more than one?"

"Yes. It's impossible for one person to be responsible for all of this."

Bruce finished reading the psyche profile report, "I think you're right about that. No one human could do this." He watched for Ferrous's response, curious about how mundane the man's knowledge really was.

The man didn't seem to have any reaction to the phrasing, instead stating in a satisfied voice. "So, you can see why this would be a bit beyond your expertise and would be better left to us?"

Bruce shrugged but decided not to argue. "I can understand that but I would still like to be kept in the loop. This is my city after all and I want to be aware of what's going on in it."

Ferrous didn't trust Bruce's nice side. That was obvious from the look on the agent's face. However, he had no ability to ban Bruce either as the local police had every right to be at the crime scenes in their cities. It also help keep down on the bad press. "We will continue to keep you apprised of developments until we leave your city."

Nodding, the detective bid him farewell and walked back out of the office, returning to his desk where Faith appeared to be sleeping.

He looked down at her. "Come on, let's get some lunch."

She lifted her head and saluted him sarcastically before standing up, sinking her hands deep into her pockets. He was surprised that she had no smart ass questions for him about his talk with Mary or where he had been but she had, honestly, been acting odd since last night. He spent the trip to the diner trying to think of how to find out what was up.

CHAPTER TWENTY-NINE

The late lunch had not gone well. Bruce had asked Faith repeatedly about the angel that had visited her and about her new attitude. He had urged her, asked her and pushed but she had given him no answers. Even more confusing, she had not even given him an argument. She had simply stared at her plate in silence, seeming to ignore him.

So Bruce had given up and they had been driving around the more rundown areas in the borders of his map of the killings, mentally checking places that might be a good hideout for a murderous angel. It took an hour before he admitted it was an exercise in futility.

Pulling into a parking lot, he turned to his passenger. "Could you please give me some kind of hint as to where this guy could be sleeping?"

Faith looked over at him. "How would I know that?"

He gritted his teeth. "Well, you had to sleep didn't you?"

She nodded. "Like eating, sleeping is something that an angel banned from heaven and hell must do."

"So where would he sleep?"

Her frown matched his. "Like I said, how should I know?"

"Because he's like you. Where did you sleep?"

She smirked at him in amusement. "You already know that." He continued to stare at her and she shook her head. "I slept how you saw. I passed out on the table. You forget, detective, I was busy being drunk. The one you're after has been busy with other things."

Bruce's grip on the steering wheel tightened. "So...who was that last night? Is he the one I'm looking for?"

She turned her head away from him, staring out the window.

He tried another tactic. "If you don't tell me, you'll stay sober longer." It was somewhat a hollow threat. He was not going to let her just fall back into the bottle if he could stop her. Like all the other burnt out cops he had seen, she deserved better than to be forgotten in a bar. However, he had no intention of her knowing that at this moment and, so, he kept his eyes firmly on the front windshield and away from her gaze.

She remained silent until he knew she wasn't going to answer. Sighing, he turned the car on and pulled onto the street, heading back towards the precinct. Before he reached his destination, though, a call came in over his phone. There had been another hit by Saint T. Claus. Bruce cursed and immediately sped in that direction, worry and confusion spurring him on. Usually, Saint T. Claus struck late at night. It was barely an hour past dark which meant either the killer was striking early for some reason such as a second target later that night or the murderer had suddenly picked up a copycat. Both of those possibilities made him very unhappy.

Pulling into the street, he could see the lights of the police cars flashing as the cops put up the crime scene tape but no reporter vans. He thought that was a bit odd and he looked around as he climbed out of the car. After a few moments study, he noticed that there really weren't any neighbors out on the street either which was very unusual with the police car lights flashing. It was a poorer section of town but that shouldn't be a factor in how clear the streets were. In fact, that usually meant the sidewalks would be even more crowded with tourists curious about what was going on.

Then, it hit him. The address was within the shadow part of town. As far as the other cops would think, it was just an insular area. The people wanting privacy more than anything, which was true. However, Bruce knew from experience that the other police present would assume the area was like this due to crime or gang presence, not the shadow races that lived here. He had found most people just made mundane excuses for the strange unless the strange got into their face and forced acknowledgment. The area also explained why the news vans hadn't arrived. Reporters liked to have crowd reactions, strong emotions, conflict for ratings. The shadow races hiding in their houses here and peering out suspiciously from behind closed shades was not good entertainment.

Looking over, he noticed Faith getting out of the car as well but said nothing as he walked to the house, ducking under the tape. He did hope that, with the target possibly being a shadow race, there would be more of a struggle and maybe a better clue this time. With that in mind, he did not even look at the victims on the floor as he walked over to the medical examiner standing next to Agent Ferrous.

"Find anything?" He did not waste time with a greeting.

The man glanced up at Bruce's approach then shook his head. "Same as the others. No prints and I'm betting the blood on the wall belongs to the two victims. Though this one did put up more of a fight. There is more evidence of a struggle than previously and I'll be checking all the blood splatters but I don't believe any of it belongs to the attackers. The only other difference is no children. These two are the youngest I've seen from this killer.

Bruce's eyes roamed over the wall, frowning at the bloody words 'I'm telling you why. Saint T. Claus is coming to town,' then down to the bodies. The woman's face was turned away from him but the male's face was visible and Bruce stared. He recognized him having seen him just the previous night.

It was one of the werewolves that had confronted him, the lead one to be specific. He looked younger lying on the floor, his back bared and blood red wings cut into his flesh.

Agent Ferrous was paying more attention than Bruce would have liked and asked, "Do you know the victim?"

Recovering quickly, Bruce shrugged. "Not really. He and his friends were causing trouble recently and I had to straighten them out. Just another young punk."

The other man nodded. "So, he'll probably have a criminal record of some kind like a large percentage of the victims." He fixed Bruce with a hard look and his voice took on a satisfied, arrogant tone. "Which is another reason I do not believe this is a transient. Such would not be able to get access to records and I do believe they are targeting these people due to what they perceive as antisocial behavior. So even if they're not accessing records, there is some way people are sharing information to pick the victims and none of that would be free."

The detective nodded a bit distractedly. "It makes sense." Internally, he thought he had figured something out. The killer was trying to teach a lesson which is why he was using this song. A song that warned people to be nice to each other.

The fibbie looked over Bruce's shoulder. "You may be using her as a consultant as you claim but I do not believe consultants should have free reign of a crime scene."

Turning, he saw Faith leaning against the wall, head down, silent. He decided to take the opportunity the complaint offered to leave. He had some things he needed to get worked out with Faith regardless of her current mood. "You're right. I'll go ahead and get her out of here." He moved to leave then paused, trying to make sure he was not acting suspiciously, and addressed the medical examiner. "Make sure I get a copy of the report." He waited for an affirmative answer and then stalked over to Faith, grabbing her arm with a growled, "Come on." He was glad she did not argue though surprised by how docile she had been behaving but didn't comment on it as they got back into his car. Quickly pulling out onto the street, he drove out towards the warehouse district where they had discussed the second victim, Amanda.

CHAPTER THIRTY

Bruce pulled into the parking lot of the abandoned warehouse and climbed out, slamming the door behind him. He had been thinking all the way from the latest victim's house and he was pretty sure he had figured some things out.

He was impatiently reaching for the handle of her door when she opened it and emerged, pushing her hood back and exposing her grey eyes, the scar along the side of her face and the mostly healed scratches from the demon. She put her hands in the sweatshirt's pocket and stared at him with an eerie calm.

"What's going on?"

She tilted her head. "Could you be any more vague?"

Bruce gritted his teeth. "I want to know where the killer is."

Grey eyes stared back at him in challenge. "And how would I know that?"

"Because you can find him. He found you so you can fucking find him." He watched her carefully, sure he was right.

She didn't deny it. She just cocked her head and asked, "Why do you think the killer found me."

"Because that was him last night and him at the soup kitchen. You told me before that you can't just tell when angels are in town, that's how you don't know who's around. However, you also told me that if you read a mortal, you can find them anywhere. I figure that goes for angels too. If you know who you're looking for and search for them, you can find them. You haven't been around an angel except that one ass at Mandy's house until last night when there was an angel in that soup kitchen and he ran…after you talked. His hearing has to be as good as yours. He heard you, didn't he? Then he disappeared and came back last night to talk to you and he's the killer." He stared hard at her. "Tell me I'm wrong. Honestly, tell me I'm wrong and I'll drop all the questions about the angel last night." She continued to stare at him in silence, obviously angry, body eerily still. "I'm right, aren't I?"

Faith turned away from and that was the confirmation he needed.

"You have to help me, Faith. Before, you didn't know who it was; all you could give me was information. But, now, you know and if you don't help me, you're an accomplice, you're helping him."

The angel turned back and glared at him. "How many times do I have to tell you, I am not responsible for anyone else? Everyone makes their own fucking decisions. Their actions are not my fault."

Bruce didn't back down. "Yes, it's his choice to kill, but it'll be your choice not to stop him, not to help me stop him, to let him keep killing. You'll choose to let the murders continue and that means you'll be partly to blame and that will be your fault."

"And so what if he does keep killing?" She was not backing down either. "Do any of the people he's killed really deserve to live? Do any of them make the world any better? They cause nothing but pain and death themselves. So, how is what he's doing a bad thing?" Her blank eyes seemed to glow with emotion but were still unreadable.

"Because he has no right to be judge, jury and executioner and he can be wrong. Even you admit angels are not all knowing, not perfect. Sure the victims are assholes now but they can change. Everyone can change."

Her voice took on a nasty cutting edge. "So, you're one of those that thinks that mass murders like Mengele don't deserve the death penalty, huh?"

Bruce shook his head, refusing to answer the ridiculous charge, recognizing it for a tactic to side track the conversation. "Don't change the subject. We're not talking about Nazi doctors here. We are talking about selfish assholes that I will agree probably need to have some sense beat into them. But that doesn't mean they deserve to die, doesn't mean they couldn't have changed if given the shot..." The image of the dead werewolf's face flashed across his thoughts. "He has no right to be the one to decide who lives and dies. He can make mistakes."

"What's your real problem here? You didn't react this bad with the others. Why are you so pissed about this one?" She stared at him suspiciously. "I thought you'd be happy about this one at least. That asshole would have killed you yesterday if I hadn't shown up."

Bruce ran his fingers through his hair but did not avoid her gaze. "Maybe, maybe not. He was a werewolf just reaching adulthood."

Faith shrugged. "So what?"

Bruce forced himself to breath in and out slowly. He had to make her understand. "Have you ever had a werewolf for a charge?"

She nodded, her expression turning into one of confusion.

"Then you should understand that the werewolf didn't deserve to be judged. Not at this age."

Her brows drew together. He had at least caught her curiosity.

"What makes you say that? Why are you bringing up his race and age?"

Bruce considered how to explain and decided to just start at the beginning. "Ok, here's a little history. I wasn't a detective when I met Tiver. He got framed by some other wererats and put in a mundane jail. I cleared him and helped him out and that was my first introduction to the shadow world. After that, I started to run into the shadow world more often…seemed like more and more of my cases took me into that part of town and I've done my best to do my job for them like I do my job for the mundane. Anyway, soon after the thing with Tiver, I ran afoul of this werewolf, same age as the one that died tonight. First time I met him, I didn't know what he was until after I stopped him mugging a businessman who left as I was cuffing the kid. I couldn't do much about the businessman, shortages in the precinct left me on my own in the car a lot. Anyway, I got the kid cuffed and he gave me this really big grin and transformed into the hybrid form, broke my cuffs, threw me into my own car, busted the window and took off. So, I invested in some silver bullets and started carrying those enchanted cuffs I have that can't be broken, the ones I used on you the first night, just in case. A few days later, I run into him again. He's causing trouble…again. I try to arrest him and he laughs at me until I put a silver bullet in his leg. Not fatal but it hurt and the threat got him into the cuffs. Where he laughed at me again, saying he could break them. He couldn't and it kept him in human form but he challenged me about what I was going to do with him. I couldn't put him in a mundane jail; they don't have the resources to deal with his race because they don't accept his race exists. So, I found out which pack he was with and I took him home to daddy who told me he'd punish the kid and thanked me for bringing him home with just the one bullet wound and for being understanding. Around a week later, I ran into the kid again, same problems only this time I had the gun on him before he hit me. Cuffed him and delivered him back to his pack again."

Faith interrupted him with a sneer. "So the dad didn't punish him after all."

Bruce shook his head. "No, he did punish him. He gave the kid a beating and the worst jobs in the den but it doesn't help when they're that age. I ran into the kid about once a week for the next month or two then he was gone. I became detective awhile after that and I didn't see the kid again until a year ago…during a prisoner transfer."

The angel laughed. "So the kid ended up in jail anyways."

He smiled as he corrected her. "No. He was the cop bringing in the prisoner for the transfer."

That surprised her. He definitely had her full attention. "What? How?"

"I asked him the same thing at lunch which he invited me too. He had asked for the transfer so he could see if I was still at the same place and he explained things to me. He told me how his father had punished him repeatedly especially as he had been actively seeking me out, seeing me as a challenge and wanting to get the better of me. According to what he said, all werewolves go through a month or two when they get overly aggressive and out of control until they're finally ready to challenge their alpha or leave the pack. He did challenge his dad and he lost, which is apparently common. Once the real challenge takes place, the werewolf calms down into their place as either part of a new pack or their home pack and they're ready to take responsibility and fulfill their role. He was going to be an alpha. His dad was grooming him to be his successor but I had apparently impressed him enough with how I handled the situation of his asshole months that he thought it'd be good for the shadow world to have people in the cops that could stand between the worlds. So, he invested in the fake papers he needed and he went into the academy and was doing his best as a cop. It wasn't easy for him either, hiding what he was. He had to take full moons off too often to get a promotion quickly but he was trying."

Faith didn't move but evenly asked, "So, he's still a cop?"

Bruce shook his head again. "Yeah. We keep in touch, help each other out when we can.

She remained silent and Bruce took a deep breath.

"Don't you see? That's why the killer had no right to hit that kid tonight. Even the most noble of werewolves is an absolute ass for a couple of months. In a couple of weeks, that kid would have done a challenge and might have settled down and been productive but we'll never know now, will we? Cause he's dead before he really had a chance to grow and if you or the killer had ever had a werewolf as a charge you should damn well know that." He stared hard at her and, for the first time he could remember, she dropped her eyes. "You do know that, don't you?"

She nodded. "I hadn't really thought about it...but yeah, I've had werewolves as charges before and yes, they're always a complete ass for a month or two."

"And the killer has had werewolf charges too, hasn't he?"

Faith nodded once again.

"Then he fucked up and you have to help me stop him."

Their eyes met as she raised her head and her voice was low and strained as she replied. "No."

CHAPTER THIRTY-ONE

"No?!" For a moment Bruce almost hit her. He really wanted to. He could not deny that. However, he didn't for two reasons. One, he did not go around just hitting people and, two, she'd probably put him in intensive care if she didn't kill him for it. He took a deep breath and tried to lower her voice below a yell. "Why not?"

She didn't drop her gaze but she did not answer either.

Bruce thought about it. "You do know who the killer is. You know they've made a mistake. Why won't you help me stop him?"

Faith sighed. "Because I don't know if he should be stopped. You're right, ok? Does that make you feel better? You're right, I know him and that was him last night. I know that the werewolf was a bad choice—"

"Bad choice? That's a great way to describe a murder."

She glared at him for his interruption. "Fine, maybe he's wrong." She held up a hand to cut off the next interruption. "Maybe. I'm not sure if he's right or wrong right now. I really don't know if there's a person on this planet that is truly worth saving. You know a few you think are so good but tell me this: Are you sure that werewolf friend of yours is so noble? He's working as a cop…but what if there are things you don't know? After all, you didn't know that Mary was a lying little bitch, did you?"

Bruce almost answered then closed his mouth and shook his head reluctantly.

"And even if he is noble, I don't know that. I really don't see this world as being worth anything or the people in it. You've all made this world a living hell…and you drove him to this."

He raised his voice again outrage. "I drove him to this? How the hell did I drive him to anything?"

Faith shook her head angrily. "Don't play word games with me. Your race and all the shadow races, you mortals drove him to murder! You broke him!"

"Who is he? If he's so fucking noble, convince me to leave him alone."

They stared at each other for a long time. "It's Samain."

"Celeste's Guardian?" Bruce was honestly shocked and Faith nodded. "How…from what you told me…" He trailed off.

"Yes, he was there during the city when they were killing their children, he's been protecting you mortals throughout history. He wrote songs of hope about all of you mortals. He even kept me from leaving service hundreds of times, showing me, showing others, that you mortals were still worth fighting for. He loved you. He held hope for this world. He still does."

"If he still has hope, why is he killing?"

"Because…" She sighed, reaching up rubbing a temple. "Because this is his hope. That with enough deaths, he'll scare you all into being nice and making this a better world."

Bruce gritted his teeth and forced himself to focus. "He's still in the wrong."

Faith shrugged. "I don't know that he is."

Grasping at a sudden inspiration, Bruce continued to argue. "But you don't know that he's right either." He paused but she didn't answer. "You aren't sure he's in the right but I'm sure he's wrong. So, just help me find him and let him and me decide who's right and who's wrong."

She stared off into the night for several moments contemplating it. "You can't fight him. You know that."

"I can fight him. I won't win in a physical fight but I can still fight him. I have to try." He sighed. "I have to stop him before he goes after another like that werewolf kid or even someone like Jasper."

She looked at him sharply and he held her gaze.

"Think about it. Jasper's violent, a criminal, even got demon possessed but he's more victim than anything else. Would that matter to Samain if they run into each other? How many others were just caught at bad times in their lives? How many has he killed that are the way they are because everyone gave up on them, because they weren't rescued? Because they weren't given the chance to become better. How many mistakes does Samain get to make before he's as bad or worse than those he's killing? I've got to get him to stop. Let me talk to him, convince him."

Faith smirked and shook her head. "You can't."

"How do you know? I convinced you to stop drinking until the end of this." He smiled as she glared at him. "What? If you really wanted to walk away and fall back into the bottle, we both know I can't really stop you. But you haven't." He stopped himself from saying more, not wanting to go too far and make her disagree out of spite.

Faith sighed and ran a hand through her gold striped hair. "Fine, I'll give you your shot. Just know something. This argument is between you and him. I'm staying out of it, completely out of it. I won't save you if you piss Samain off enough to kill you."

Bruce felt a shiver of fear and disappointment run down his spine but he was already resolved to see this through. "Just take me to him."

She climbed back into the car and closed her eyes for a moment as he walked around the hood and got into the driver's seat. Opening her eyes, she pointed to the east. "That direction." He looked at her suspiciously and she shrugged. "This is not a phone directory I'm using. I can't just give his exact current street address. He's that way; you'll get more as we get closer."

Bruce pulled out onto the street and headed east.

CHAPTER THIRTY-TWO

They traveled in silence for awhile, Faith indicating any needed changes of heading. This was giving Bruce time to think about what he was planning to do and that was a very bad thing. He could feel the fear growing inside him as his logical side explained exactly how stupid he was being.

He was on his way to argue with a broken angel not bound by the rules that would usually keep Bruce alive. Granted, he had already argued with Faith several times but she'd shown she was not going to kill him for being annoying. This one he was going to face, though, made a habit of killing people for being stupid or asses.

Unfortunately, there was no one else to stand against Samain. Bruce had sworn to do everything he could to defend the people of this city and Bruce was a man of his word so, stupid or not, he had to go and try.

That did not mean, however, that he wasn't afraid so he decided to try to distract himself and the only option for that was Faith.

He began with the first topic that occurred to him. "So what is it with you and Samain anyway? Is he an ex-boyfriend or something?"

Faith gave a surprised laugh. "No, unlike mortal fantasies, in reality, angels do not engage in romance or sex. He is my dearest friend and was my best student but there was no erotic love there."

"No sex?" That surprised him. "So new angels are never born? That's why your numbers are so low?"

"Turn a bit more south. No, new angels are formed but we're not mortal and we don't reproduce like you. Turn left. Why would we?"

Bruce followed the directions, curious now and glad for the distraction. "So, then, how…"

Faith shrugged "Not fully sure. Never really cared enough to think about it. Just every once in awhile, there's a new one that is given to an older angel to mentor."

"So, you never have sex at all?" Bruce tapped impatiently on the wheel waiting for a light to turn green.

The angel laughed again. "You say that like it's some horrible punishment but, no, we can't. A little more north."

"Can't?" The detective smirked. "Don't you mean won't?"

He could sense her roll her eyes. "No, I mean can't. Angels and mortals are different. We're not just humans with wings. So why would we have organs and shit we don't need?"

Bruce laughed as a thought occurred to him. "So that angel, Shh—whatever, the one at Mandy's house, he's dickless?"

"Turn right. I guess. I hadn't ever thought about it."

Another thought occurred to him. "If you don't reproduce, why do you even look like men and women and even refer to each other by he and she?"

"Because it makes us more familiar to mortals. You people are so race centric, you assign gender to cars. Anything without a gender makes you people freak out and you'd never listen…not that you listen now…but gender really means nothing to us. Otherwise, why would I have male charges? It would be real fucking creepy angels having charges of both genders if we actually had any interest in romance and gender or any of your hormones and desire to breed and such. More problems than there are already are. Turn right here."

Bruce slowed the car as he considered what she had said but he soon had to focus on the road instead. They were headed deeper into the shadow world area of the city and the streets were dangerous with debris and potholes.

Finally, Faith told him to pull over. They got out and she led him into a dark alleyway between two abandoned buildings. At the end of the dark path, there was a square that used to be the foundation of an apartment building but it had been burned out leaving the front intact and parts of the side walls and floors clinging to the corners but the rest was an open space bounded on all sides by other dark apartment buildings. They stepped out from the alleyway and there was immediate movement above them from one of the precarious corner perches. A man leapt down, landing in a crouch in front of them. He had on heavy boots, ripped jeans and an oversized sweatshirt. The hood was back, fully exposing all grey eyes and two sword hilts were visible over his shoulders, shining brighter as his wings burst forth. Standing, he was about Bruce's height though leaner of build and his long silver and gold hair was swept back into a ponytail. His face was full of confusion as he looked between Faith and Bruce but there seemed to be a gleam of hope as well.

He smiled at Faith. "Greetings, Krrna. Have you changed your mind?"

Faith shook her head and there was a brittle quality to her voice. "No. I still want nothing to do with this. I want to be left alone, to forget."

"Then…why are you here? And why bring the human?" The look he turned on Bruce was not friendly.

"He's the cop assigned to your killings. He wants you to stop."

Samain frowned. "And you've come to plead his case for him?" Hurt betrayal shone on his face.

Faith gritted her teeth and shook her head emphatically. "No. I'm done with both of you. You two fucking work this out for yourselves. Neither of you listen anyways." She walked over to a still standing wall and leaned back against it, crossing her arms over her chest.

CHAPTER THIRTY-THREE

Samain and Bruce stared at each other for several moments, sizing each other up.

It was the angel that broke the silence first. "What is it you want?"

Bruce tried his most reasonable tone. "I want you to stop killing people."

Samain tilted his head in curiosity. "Why?"

Bruce gritted his teeth. Why was it that the answer only seemed obvious to him? "Because it's wrong. You're murdering these people."

The angel shook his head and his face took on an expression of patience as if Bruce was a simpleton. "I'm not murdering…I'm teaching a lesson."

The detective took a calming breath, trying to ignore the angel's tone. "You're still wrong, whatever your reasons. Killing helpless people is wrong. Period."

Samain gave a derisive laugh, "Who says I'm wrong? You?"

Bruce appealed to the best authority he could. "Yes and God said it too."

The angel's eyes narrowed in offended anger. "You claim to speak with God? You dare?" His hand reached back for a sword.

The detective wanted to curse angel stubbornness and misunderstandings. "No, I'm not claiming that. But I've heard the Ten Commandments. They're in the bible, God's word, and they say Thou shalt not kill."

Samain shrugged it off. "That was a rule given to man, not angels. Besides, it was actually thou shalt not murder."

Bruce glared at him, quickly running out of patience, "Fine. It's only a law for humans but I know a bit about angel law. You're a guide and a guardian. You're not allowed to be judge and executioner. It's forbidden, isn't it?"

Samain's derisive smile was almost an exact duplicate of Faith's usual expression. It emphasized the long relationship between the two broken angels. "I quit. Didn't Krrna tell you? Rules don't apply when you quit."

The human shook his head. "The rules still apply, you're just breaking them. That's why you can't go to heaven or hell."

The angel took a step forward, anger beginning to show on his face.

"Fine, I am breaking the rules. But the rules are no good any longer. They don't work. They don't protect the innocent. They tie our hands from doing what needs to be done."

Bruce did not give ground, stubborn even in the face of the other's growing annoyance. "Fine, your system is flawed. I won't argue that. Our own system is flawed so I understand your frustration. I really do. You can see my eyes. You can read how many times I've bent the rules to put someone away, how many times I've wanted to say to hell with the system and become like you, judge, jury and executioner but I don't."

"Because you're a coward." The words were spat out in disgust.

"Wrong. It's because I know we have to have rules. We have to have a system. Without that, it's chaos. Everyone does as they please. If I did that, I would have killed innocent people. I would have just shot the most likely suspect instead of investigating and finding out that most likely doesn't mean is. The system forces me to do it right and it fucks up, yeah, but better than absolute chaos with no accountability." Bruce paused as a thought occurred to him. "And isn't that what Armageddon will truly be? A breakdown into chaos. Angels and demons doing whatever they want, battling in the streets, killing on impulse or 'gut feeling'? Everyone acting like you and burning the world in your own private war."

"It is a holy mission and I would never make the mistake of punishing the wrong person. I can see the corruption and maliciousness of their hearts, their selfishness and cruelty"

"Reading someone's heart doesn't make you all knowing. It doesn't let you see the future. They could have changed. They could have learned but you took that chance away from them for, basically, misdemeanors."

The angel shook his head. "They were corrupt at heart and the heart never changes."

Bruce smirked. It wasn't a good idea but he couldn't help it. "Bullshit. You and Faith are proof that hearts can change. You were both guardians, completely dedicated to protecting from what I've heard. Now, it's all changed. You're a murderer and she doesn't care about anyone. If you could change in your hearts, so could they and they weren't evil. They were assholes but that's not the same as evil."

Samain growled in a rage, lunging forward impossibly fast and catching the detective by the throat, bodily lifting him into the air. His sword was poised to strike and Bruce instinctively drew his gun, even though it was probably useless. "Enough! You are mortal and can not understand." He stared hard into the human's eyes.

Bruce glanced over at Faith. She had not moved from her place leaning on the wall, arms still crossed over her chest, passively watching.

"She already said this is not her fight, human." Bruce's eyes snapped back to Samain's ash grey gaze. "However, I see that you are indeed benevolent. You are not part of the cancer I seek to excise but you are attempting to thwart me all the same. Give me your word that you will no longer interfere and I will allow you to live. I will even give you a gift. After I finish my task here, I will leave your city and not to return to it within your lifetime. Continue to oppose me, however, and I will kill you here and now and I will make sure to return here every year. Your city will be my greatest canvas."

Bruce knew Samain meant it and the offer was tempting. He did not want to die and another glance at Faith showed that she was as disinterested in the proceedings as ever. However, it was a hollow gift that he was offered. Bruce might save the people of this city by taking the bribe but every time he heard of Samain's next round of victims, he'd know that he had sold them out for his own life. He was a cop, a guardian. He really only had one choice.

Raising his arm, he aimed the pistol at Samain's left eye. "If good men stand by and do nothing, evil flourishes."

"You're a dead man."

"I know." Bruce pulled the trigger.

Samain's head tilted to the side with inhuman speed and the bullet flew past his head. The bright sword was descending toward Bruce's chest.

He blinked.

He was still breathing, no pain.

Faith was there between them. Her hand was wrapped around Samain's wrist stopping the descent of the sword. Her wings glowed brightly and one was curled around Bruce, somehow supporting him, warm and not the burning heat he'd felt from them before.

"Krrna, what—"

"He's willing to die to protect them. He's seen their worst but he still protects them. I will stand his guardian." Her voice was soft but firm.

Samain stared at her, his face pleading. "I don't want to fight you, harm you. Don't do this."

"Then relent, Samain. I stand his guardian." Her voice was stronger though still emotionless.

"Don't make me do this!" He was begging. "You have no swords, no weapons at all. You'll die."

If Faith was moved or afraid, it didn't show in her voice. "You have free will as do I. Nothing is forced. I choose to guard this man. What do you choose?"

Samain's hand released Bruce who would have fallen but for the wing wrapped around him. Faith set him down onto his feet without looking back at him, her eyes focused on Samain.

As the killer stepped back away from Faith, the human could see tears on his face, glistening in the light of their wings but his expression had hardened. "So be it. I will mourn you for eternity, Krrna."

He fell into a ready stance, drawing his other sword as Faith crouched low, hands spread.

Bruce felt strong hands grab his jacket yanking him back and he struggled until he heard Tiver's voice. "Stop that. Crazy human. Gotta get you out of their way before they kill you by accident."

Startled, Bruce stopped resisting as the wererat pulled him back to a nearby wall. Waiting there were several werewolves in their hybrid forms.

"What the hell?" That was the best Bruce could come up with in that moment.

Tiver glanced back at them. "The dead werewolf kid...well, meet his parents and you already met his two brothers there. Saw you driving through town but not to the bar, figured you were after the killer. They were there and offering a reward for the guy. So...took a bit to track your ass down. Told them to give up, that they were hunting an angel, but..."

"We didn't believe him." The large male werewolf's voice rumbled like thunder.

Bruce nodded but lost all interest in their presence as he focused on the fight.

One of Samain's swords cut deep through Faith's wing and it bled rainbow colored plasma even as she ducked under his guard and came up with a hard palm strike to his jaw, rocking him back and away from her.

"Oh god, he's going to kill her." Without a sword, Bruce didn't see how she was going to survive, much less win. "We've gotta help her."

A glowing blade swept through the space her neck had been a half second before.

"And how're we gonna to do that? Sorry, but I forgot to bring my arrow of fucking powerful creature slaying tonight." Tiver's sarcasm was not welcome at that moment even if he had a point.

Faith's wings flared out as she dodged back from Samain's renewed assault and she took to the air and Samain followed her up. She managed a rolling twisting maneuver that put her behind him and her foot lashed out, catching him in the spine and knocking him through into a wall. Bruce thought he heard a bone break but, if he was right, it wasn't enough to stop the killer. Samain pushed away from the brick, slashing furiously at her midsection and their fight went higher into the air as they swooped and spun for position, moving faster now so that they were becoming blurs of light through the sky. It was hard to follow the action but he could tell Faith was on the defensive, evading the swords but unable to attack.

Then, suddenly, Samain got a good shot of some kind in because Faith hit a wall hard enough to crack the bricks before slamming down to the concrete with a bone jarring thud. She tried to push herself up but her left arm gave way, her shoulder crashing to the ground again.

Samain landed close to her, swords lowered as he approached. "I regret this, Krrna."

Faith tried again and managed to push herself up into a half crouch, face twisted in pain. "Just fucking do it. I won't yield."

His voice was sorrowful but resigned. "I'll make it quick."

Bruce was already moving forward as Samain thrust the sword forward. He had no plan in mind but he had to do something even though he knew angels were too fast and he was too far away.

Faith suddenly dodged and spun as the blade went through her, the momentum of her twisting body enough to pull the hilt from Samain's grip. She stilled several feet away and Bruce could see the sword had pieced her left side. It was not a killing blow but it had to hurt like hell.

With a vicious looking smile, she unsheathed the sword from her own flesh. "I always told you, don't assume how hurt they are. Be prepared."

Samain growled in anger at being tricked, switching his remaining blade into his other hand and attacking again.

Brilliant sparks filled the air as the swords met again and again. It was a different fight now that they were both armed. Faith was no longer retreating and Bruce was reminded of laser light shows as their movements sped up until their forms were nothing but indistinct blurs of light once again, too fast to follow.

He didn't realize he was holding his breath when one crashed to the earth like a comet. It took a moment for his eyes to clear enough to realize it was Samain. The angel was struggling to rise but Faith didn't give him the time to recover. She dropped down onto his stomach with both feet, holding her blade downward so it pierced his chest before she leapt away again.

Samain didn't even have time to make a sound before his eyes turned an unseeing black and his body caught fire, becoming ash in a matter of seconds.

There was a silent moment as they all stared down at the grey dust form that had been an angel seconds before then Faith fell to her knees, throwing her head back in a long wordless scream.

CHAPTER THIRTY-FOUR

The scream still hung in the air when Faith let her head fall forward onto her chest, hair hiding her face as she knelt there, golden blood still running down her wing and side but dissipating as it hit the ground. Bruce moved forward cautiously, not sure of her state of mind though she was an image of desolate sorrow. Not that he blamed her. She had just killed her best friend and, since it was because of him, Bruce wasn't sure how safe he was but he still had to check on her.

He had just reached her side when there was a firm cold voice behind him.

"Step away from the abomination, mortal."

Bruce mentally cursed. He knew that voice and he did not need a still official guardian angel right now. Turning, he saw Shrrrel hovering between the buildings, sword drawn, wings gleaming and staring past him at Faith.

The detective took a step, placing himself more in front of Faith and blocking the other angel's view. "What do you want here?"

The angel's gaze was hard, his eyes shining with swirling rainbows. "I have come to kill the abomination."

Bruce did not back down. A small part of him was actually getting used to this and the rest of him was pretty sure that fact was proof he needed to be in a straightjacket. "There is no abomination here."

Shrrrel's expression became colder. "Do not seek to defend her. I felt the death of the angel at her hands. I have come to execute her for one of the highest of crimes."

Bruce crossed his arms, his anger over Samain's stubbornness boiling to the top. "She executed the killer, Saint T. Claus, the one you should have stopped. If you could sense his death, why didn't you just sense him out and stop him yourself?"

The angel landed, stepping forward and part of Bruce wondered if Faith would save him from this sword. "It is not your place to question, mortal, but, since I believe this abomination has lied to you as her kind is wont to do, I will explain. I was not aware there was an angel in the city except this one. I had not attained permission to investigate the killings when last we met; I had other things to take care of. Now, I have come to deal with this problem only to feel an angel die in the city. That is something unmistakable. I have come to end her threat."

Bruce felt his muscles tense in anger. The arrogance was really getting too much for him. "She's not the one that did it. If you'd paid any attention like you should have, you'd know that. She stopped the broken angel that did it."

Shrrrel seemed a little taken aback by his outburst and the detective had a small hope that the angel had been convinced. However, the next comment made Bruce realize he was too much of an optimist. "You would speak so to me? A guardian that has served faithfully for five centuries now? And how do you mean, broken? There is no such thing as a broken angel."

The human glared at the shining immortal. "Yes there is but you're so blinded by your self righteousness you can't see it. Samain didn't fall and neither did Faith. They broke under the strain and you should have come after them and helped them, not let them fall through the cracks until they came to this. You should have done something before this. But you didn't and you're sure as hell not going to do anything now. Leave her the fuck alone and get the hell out of here."

Shrrrel took another step forward, raising his shining sword. "You sinner! You shall be chastised for this!"

The logical part of his mind screamed for Bruce to run or fall to his knees and beg for mercy. The problem solving part of his mind grasped tightly on what he had learned, feeding him a way out. He stared confidently at the advancing angel. "You can't hurt me. You have no right. I am not supernatural. I am not a threat to other humans."

The angel gritted his teeth then growled, "But you stand in the way of the punishment of a supernatural evil. Therefore, I may remove you by any means that I deem necessary."

Bruce shook his head with a grin of triumph. "No, you can't. She is not a supernatural threat to mortals. She killed the threat and she is no threat to any mortal present. By your own laws, you have no rights to her or to me."

He felt a presence at either side of him but did not dare take his eyes from Shrrrel but realized the werewolves had moved forward when the alpha spoke out beside him. "He's right. She killed the murdering renegade, avenging my son and preventing the deaths of others. Your kind can hunt us in the shadows when we cross the line but even we know you can't kill a mortal when there's no immortal threat and there's no threat to mortals here."

Shrrrel seethed with fury, his wings pulsating. "You're lying."

The werewolf was calm. "Soul read us, angel, and you will see it's truth."

The angel's gaze bored hard into each of the mortals but he finally sheathed the sword, though reluctantly. "Very well, you tell the truth." He glared at Bruce. "Watch your step well, human. You are misguided and travel into dark ways. I will remember this and you." Between one breath and the next, he was gone.

Bruce let out a breath he had been holding then turned to the werewolves. "Thanks for the back up."

The large male nodded down from his eight foot height. "You are welcome. I owed you and her for avenging my son…and for the trouble he and my sons tried to cause you." He glared over at two of the other furred humanoids who lowered their heads respectfully under his admonishing gaze. "They will not bother you again." He raised his voice towards his sons. "Will you?"

The two large males both softly voiced their agreement.

Bruce nodded but was careful not to smile in amusement. Instead, he simply thanked them again and watched as they slipped away. He next turned to Tiver, thanking him as well.

The wererat responded in his usual way, shrugging and stating, "Yeah, well remember, you owe me."

The detective nodded, acknowledging the debt. "Yeah, and you know I'll pay up."

Tiver nodded. "Yeah, I know, bye." He followed the wolves into the alleyways.

That left Bruce alone with Faith. She wouldn't look at him but she had both of Samain's swords on the ground in front of her as she pulled his scabbards from the ash that had been his body.

"I'm surprised those scabbards survived, nothing else did." Bruce wanted to take back the words as they were past his lips, realizing how insensitive they were.

Her voice was quiet and somehow empty as she answered. "The scabbards are built to withstand our wings in the full fury of battle. They are as strong as the swords."

Bruce licked his lips, trying to think of what else to say. Sorry just didn't seem enough but he had to try. "I…I'm sorry you had to kill Samain."

She snorted. "Haven't I taught you a damn thing? The fight with him was my choice, my responsibility.

Bruce was a bit taken aback by her words but knew he should have expected them. "I…I still appreciate that you helped me."

Faith strapped on the scabbards and sheathed the swords across her back then looked at him for the first time since Samain had died. Bruce wondered if it was the light of her still glowing wings but he thought her eyes were a little less flat grey than before. However, he couldn't be sure and she was speaking again.

"Don't think you saved me."

Bruce blinked. "What?"

"Don't you dare think you saved me from Shrrrel. I had swords this time. He's a hell of a lot younger than me and I can beat him. Always could. You saved him, not me."

The detective smiled. "Hey, I believe you."

He would have said more but Faith interrupted him. "And just cause it was my choice to face Samain and you faced off against Shrrrel, don't you dare think you and I are done. I will still have my pound of flesh from you for making me sober and getting me involved in all this shit."

"About that…"

She glared at him. "What?"

Bruce took a deep breath. "Don't go back into the bottle."

"Why not?" Her eyes bored into his in challenge. "What the fuck do you care what I do now? Your city is safe…well safer. The killer is dead."

He held her gaze trying to find the right words. "Because you're not as uncaring as you say and because you could do so much but most of all because I don't want to see you wasting your life away in the bottle. The world needs you."

She tilted her head, considering, looking through him, he knew, into his soul. "But do I need the world?"

He opened his mouth to argue with her again but she was already gone.

CHAPTER THIRTY-FIVE

It had been a week since Bruce had seen any angels and things were mostly back to normal. Mary was still his partner though there had been some very tense moments when he had come back with the case closed and no one arrested. However, she had backed him with both the sergeant and the fibbies when he had told them that he was stumped on this case and left it to them to realize the deaths had stopped and move on. What else could he do? They would never believe what had really happened. He had no proof other than Saint T. Claus did not strike again.

He hoped that Mary and he could rebuild their partnership and it seemed she was hoping the same but the easy rapport there had once been was gone. He no longer gave her his passwords and she no longer chatted with him. However, she was still there and that was the important part to him.

Though, technically, at the moment, she wasn't in her chair. She had gone out to get them lunch while he worked on some paperwork.

As he filled out what seemed to be the exact same form for the sixth time, Bruce caught movement out of the corner of his eye and looked up. Standing there by his desk, shifting nervously from foot to foot, was Jasper. The man looked like he was ready to rabbit at any moment so Bruce made sure to keep his voice soft and even as he asked, "Can I help you?"

"Depends…maybe…uh…." Jasper's tone was ranging from defiant to unsure. Bruce calmly waited and the younger man licked his lips. "You're….Are you Detective Bruce?"

"Yeah. Would you like to sit down?" He indicated the chair next to his desk.

Jasper nodded and sat down, fidgeting but silent again.

Bruce decided to try to jumpstart the conversation. "How can I help you, Jasper?"

The younger man's head shot up. "You…you know me?"

"I was there when you tried to take credit for the Saint T. Claus murders." He didn't see a reason to lie.

Jasper peered at him but there was no recognition. "I guess but…I…I was pretty messed up then. I don't—"

"Don't worry about it. Just tell me how I can help you now."

"Well…you're not gonna believe me…if you seen my record, you're just gonna think I was high or something but I wasn't. It happened and you gotta help me." His voice was taking a panicked edge.

Bruce put a comforting hand on his shoulder which also kept the slimmer man in place. "Calm down. I can believe a lot more than you think. Just tell me what happened and I'll see if I can help."

Jasper licked his lips nervously again. "Well, see I was…I was going to go buy some stuff from a dealer." He stared at Bruce suspiciously.

The detective shook his head a little. "I know you've got a history of drug use. But you came to me for help. I'm not going to just run you in for telling me you were doing a drug buy."

"That's the thing though…I didn't buy anything. I was going to, I was going through the shakes and everything…but…Before I could, this woman appeared out of like nowhere. She had these blazing wings and she beat the dealer bloody then grabbed my arm and dragged me off. She told me to come to this precinct and ask for a detective named Bruce…and…" His voice suddenly turned desperate and his words spilled out faster. "I wasn't hallucinating, I wasn't on anything. She was really there."

The detective tightened his grip comfortingly and nodded. "It's ok, Jasper. I believe you."

The younger man stared at him hard, suspicious of being made fun of but Bruce actually did believe him so the sincerity showed on his face. Finally, Jasper seemed to accept that. "Ok…well…she said to find this detective named Bruce…you… and that you'd help me out. That you'd get me in rehab and off the streets…said to tell you I was her pound of flesh, whatever that fucking means."

Bruce smiled and nodded, somehow not really surprised at the information. "Yeah. I'll help you out. If you really want to get off the drugs and get off the street, I'll help you." He reached for his rolodex looking for the number to a state run rehab center that would accept Jasper.

The younger man smiled in relief. "Good, cause she gave me another message for you."

He glanced up at him. "Oh? What was it?"

"She told me that she was gonna check up on me at odd times in the future and if she found me on the streets again she was gonna kick my ass and then she was gonna come after yours."

Bruce laughed softly. It was so typically Faith.

Jasper misinterpreted his amusement and leaned in closer. "Dude, she meant it. You didn't see her. She was real and she meant it."

The detective looked up with a reassuring smile. "I believe you. I know her and I'm not laughing at you, I'm laughing because I know she meant every word."

ABOUT THE AUTHOR

Dara Hannon lives in the US with her two cats. When relaxing, she enjoys reading, doing crafts and MMORPGs. She admits to being a coffee addict who can't stand the taste of espresso.

Look for these books
from Blue Oranda Publishing
in your favorite e-bookstore

By Harry Heckel

<u>Crimson Hawks Adventures</u>
In the Service of the King
Cinders and Ashes (Coming Soon)

<u>Krueger Chronicles</u>
Souls of the Everwood
Black Powder and Brimstone (Coming Soon)

Charming (with John Peck) (Coming Soon)

By Brad A. White

Servant of the Muses

By Wayland Smith

In My Brother's Name

www.ingramcontent.com/pod-product-compliance
Lightning Source LLC
Chambersburg PA
CBHW070927130626
46555CB00001B/317